SWEETHEART SUMMER

(A Cranberry Bay Novel #2)

by

Mindy Hardwick

EAGLE BAY PRESS

Cover design by Self-Publishing Services LLC
    (MK McClintock)
Developmental Edit by Bev Katz Rosenbaum,
Copy Edit by Self-Publishing Services LLC (Clare Wood)
Formatted by Self-Publishing Services LLC.
    (www.Self-Publishing-Service.com)

Eagle Bay Press
Lake Stevens, Washington

For my Mom

Table of Contents

Sweetheart Summer
Acknowledgements

This story was not easy to write, and it took a team of people to keep me going when I wanted to quit. Thank you to the Starbucks in Frontier Village Shopping Center in Lake Stevens, Washington, which kept me in mocha Frappuccinos and served as my office for a good majority of the writing of the last draft. Laurie Glass and our weekly dinner brainstorming sessions brought the story back to life every time it was dying. Kathy Mackal's beach walks with the dogs and enthusiasm for reading the book kept me going on the days I wanted to quit. And to Jim Stallcup who encouraged me to write through to the last page.

The story's setting never would have been written without the north Oregon coast towns of Wheeler and Nehalem. Thank you for sharing your beautiful area with me.

The team who works with me to bring my romance books to publication is fabulous, and I am lucky to have all of you. Thank you to the amazing developmental editing of Bev Katz Rosenbaum, the fine copyediting of Clare Wood, and, especially, thanks to Danica Winters and her team at SPS Self-Publishing LLC. Thank you so much for always keeping me in great covers!

As always, the Greater Seattle RWA Chapter is invaluable to my growth as a writer and encourages me to take new risks and explore new options.

My very best writer pal, Rhay Christou, dealt with more of my off the page drama during the writing of this book than anyone should ever be asked to handle. My best love to you, dear friend. I am forever in your debt for this one.

And especially thank you to my sweet contemporary readers who with their support and belief in my romantic storytelling encouraged me to keep telling the stories of Cranberry Bay.

Chapter One

"There are no bids for Sawyer's handyman service?" Jack Perkins frowned. His top hat slanted as the lawyer looked at the crowded circular tables in the riverboat's lower room. The citizens of Cranberry Bay averted their eyes as they devoured slices of thick strawberry cheesecake, rhubarb pie, and lemon meringue cake.

At the back of the room, Katie smoothed her hands over her knit skirt and crossed and uncrossed her legs under the rectangular table. Beside her, the elementary school's PTA secretary, Beth Dawson, scribbled on a large tablet of yellow paper as she added up auction services and prices. Katie fiddled with her pencil, and her stomach contracted. She'd known when the items came in for the auction; this would be the reaction to Sawyer's offer. The only thing she hadn't counted on was sitting beside his ten-year-old daughter, Lauren, and watching her respond to her dad's unpopularity.

"Why doesn't anyone want to bid on Dad?" Lauren whispered and tugged on the pink ribbon cascading down the side of her sundress. She wiggled in the metal folding chair beside Katie and rubbed her thumb over a long column of scribbled numbers on large lined paper. A small pink glob of bubblegum moved to the corner of her mouth as she chewed hard.

Katie bit her lower lip and took a deep breath. She often imagined the young girl, who lived next door, was the daughter she could never have. The last thing she wanted was to see her hurt. "Your Dad is talented," she began. No one in

Cranberry Bay or the surrounding Oregon coast communities could deny it. Sawyer was a great local developer. His premier second-home beach development showcased state-of-the-art designs and features. He'd also been featured in national magazines and trade shows for years.

But how did she explain to Lauren that Sawyer's last project, developing a subdivision on a sloped hill, resulted in two years' worth of battles among the city's attorneys, the council, and the residents of Cranberry Bay? How did she explain that long-timers did not want their town to turn into a market of expensive homes crowded together on small lots? More than one person muttered that the oldest Shuster brother, Sawyer, had lost his family's understanding of small town life and was being driven by greed.

Katie had worked tirelessly spearheading a group of locals to fight Sawyer's plans every step of the way. She loved the small town where she and her mother had sought safety from her abusive father when she was twelve. The last thing she wanted to see was it ruined by selfish indulgent development. But each time, Sawyer's team of lawyers had convinced the council to move forward. Finally, the devastated citizens admitted defeat and sadly watched as the bulldozers moved in and broke ground on land overlooking the river.

Lauren chewed hard on her gum. She fiddled with a large blue button on her pastel blue cardigan. "Why is no one bidding on him?"

Katie's heart ached. She knew all too well what it was like to have a Dad who was a source of small-town shame. Her Dad had so often became violent after his nightly glasses of Scotch, reaching for her or her mother to vent his anger. Often, she lay in bed, shaking, as her mother's screams filled the small house. The next morning, Katie pretended everything was fine. She covered the bruises with long sleeves and wore caps pulled over her eyes so no one could see her face. She waved away all offers of help from well-meaning schoolteachers and neighbors, but the pit of fear in her stomach never subsided after she returned home at the end of the day.

Desperate to do something to stop Lauren's distress, Katie looked around the room for her four best friends, the women of the Cranberry Bay sewing circle. Immediately, she caught Rylee's eye. Rylee frowned, and she tapped a black high-heeled foot under the table. Her black sequined dinner dress sparkled as the setting May sun shone through the open windows of the boat.

Rylee nodded to Katie and lifted her paddleboard. Her new engagement ring twinkled in the light, and beside her, the middle Shuster, Bryan, dropped his arm lightly around her chair. "Two-hundred dollars," Rylee's clear voice called. Bryan leaned over, his eyes caressing her as he smiled deep into her eyes. His tie, covered with small boats, grazed the edge of the table. The sewing circle women had scoured the shops in Portland for hours, helping Rylee find the perfect gift for the grand opening of Bryan's riverboat. Bryan moved his hand along the back of Rylee's shoulders and squeezed gently.

Katie's heart skipped a beat. She longed for someone who could feel so much tenderness toward her and to whom she could respond with the same glowing smile Rylee gave Bryan. But her short marriage to Marc had shown her how easily love slipped into pain and heartache when he spiraled into a heroin addiction fed by prescription drugs after hip surgery. The drugs had stolen the man she once loved and turned him into an emotionally abusive monster. The last she had heard, Marc lived on the streets of Seattle, and she had quietly shut off that part of her that wanted to believe in "happily ever after."

"Do I hear two fifty?" Jack's dark eyes sparkled as he pushed a lock of thick gray hair from his forehead.

Ivy, Cranberry Bay antique shop owner and sewing circle member, lifted her paddleboard. "Two hundred fifty." Her sparkling red-and-pink headband held back her long, thick, dark hair. Her long paisley skirt draped to the floor, and a pink shawl was tossed over her shoulders. She wore an antique silver necklace, which rested lightly on a pale peach top with spaghetti straps.

"Three hundred?" Jack gazed around the room.

The room stilled, but no more bids were forthcoming.

"That's all?" Lauren asked. "The ugly glass vase got a lot more bids than Dad." Her lower lip trembled.

"Let me see what I can do." Katie raised her paddleboard. "Three hundred." She gritted her teeth. Sawyer was the last person she wanted to bid on. But she didn't want Lauren to hurt over her dad's unpopularity either. The little girl adored her father.

Lauren pressed her warm body against Katie. Katie's chest contracted with a deep longing. She had never been able to have children, and Marc constantly reminded her of that fact. She had tried to pretend it didn't bother her and threw herself into volunteering at after-school craft clubs, teaching summer sewing camps, and spending hours with young sewers in her shop.

When her aunt and uncle decided to retire and move to Florida, they'd sold part of their dairy farm to Sawyer. Katie had been devastated, knowing the day would come when Sawyer would turn the beautiful farmland into a small-home development. But when Ginger, Sawyer's wife and Lauren's mother, passed away, Lauren sought solace from Katie. The two spent hours baking cookies, playing games, and watching movies. Each of them seeking to fill a missing need in the other.

"Three hundred," Jack said. "Going once. Going twice. Sold! To Ms. Katie Coos."

Katie lowered the paddleboard. Her hand shook, and she grabbed the pencil to steady it. The last thing she could afford was a three hundred dollar bid for Sawyer's work. The fabric shop, given to her to run after her mother died of cancer, skated close to the edge of being able to pay its bills each month. She'd have to do some advertising for consignment sewing to cover her costs this month and hope that one of the owners of a second home at the beach wanted a new fabric covering on a couch or patio set.

"That's your bid!" Beth adjusted her bifocals. She scribbled down Katie's name, the item, and bid amount on the tablet in front of her.

"I want to add the numbers to our tally." Lauren pressed hard on her pencil and frowned. Her mouth moved as she counted numbers on her left hand.

Beth pushed the tablet toward Lauren as Sawyer stepped up to the table.

"You're adding by hand?" His deep, smooth, sensual voice dropped into Katie's stomach. At six feet two, Sawyer had a commanding presence. His muscular build and dark eyes caused her insides to turn over in small shivers that she quickly pushed aside, remembering that the man was a ruthless developer who cared nothing for the town she loved and the people who made Cranberry Bay home.

"Katie bid on your services!" Lauren jumped up and wrapped her arms around Sawyer in a large bear-hug. "You could help her develop a house and a garden. Just like ours. And we could have matching houses."

"I think that might be a little much for this project," Sawyer's smooth voice said. His eyes never left Katie's as he rubbed Lauren's head. "I saw what you did." He lowered his voice to a cool frosty tone. "I don't need your pity."

"I didn't ..." Katie pressed her lips together. There was no point trying to explain to Sawyer why she had bid on his services. He'd never understand how his actions had consequences that rippled to the people around him.

Jack slapped his hand on the gravel podium and pointed to Ivy. "One family pass to Cranberry Bay's Santa Train's Midnight Excursion."

Ivy flushed and waved her paddle number toward Katie. Everyone in the sewing circle knew Ivy had bid on Josh because she harbored secret feelings for her longtime friend. But Katie eyed Josh as he stood by the refreshment table and whispered something to town's mayor, Doug Mays. He didn't even look at Ivy. Katie shook her head. Josh never seemed aware of Ivy's feelings.

Sawyer leaned over and tapped the paper in front of Katie. His left arm brushed against her side, and she held herself straight and rigid so as not to feel the shivers of attraction. "These numbers are not correct." He reached into the pocket of his dark dress pants and pulled out a slick black cell phone. "Use the calculator app."

Katie waved away the offer, being careful not to touch any part of the muscular body beside her. Why did Sawyer always need to insist people do things his way? Thankfully, after the slope-homes fiasco, the town had elected a few new council members who weren't so enamored of Sawyer's lawyers. He had been forced to scale back his latest commercial development, Liberty Bay Square, because of protected wetlands on the property. Even so, the threat to the small town's Main Street shops had kept Katie and the Small Business Association worried about losing their business to big-box stores, which could offer discounts and coupons they couldn't.

"Adding numbers by hand is not efficient for an auction." Sawyer lifted an eyebrow. "And," he looked down at her, his gaze unreadable, "you'll be up all night working on it." He set the phone in front of her. His fingers grazed her left elbow, and against her will, shivers tumbled around her stomach. Katie clenched her teeth.

"Ivy won the bid for the family pass for the holiday train ride?" Beth waved her calligraphy pen in the air as she reached for a gold-embossed certificate from a stack beside her.

"The items on the certificates should have been done on a computer," Sawyer muttered. His voice filled with disapproval.

Katie straightened and threw her shoulders back. "Beth likes working on the certificates," she said. "She is a gifted calligrapher. And Lauren is practicing her math skills by helping us."

"None of it is efficient," Sawyer said darkly beside her left ear.

"Did you give us your check?" Beth turned and asked Katie. She averted her eyes from Sawyer. Beth's home had been affected by Sawyer's slope development. Construction of the homes had damaged the roots of the pink cherry trees she'd planted when her husband passed away. When they finished building, the tall homes, perched on top of garages to ensure commanding views of the river, had stolen the sweeping view Beth had enjoyed for over thirty years. Now, she always kept her living room curtains closed to avoid looking directly at the back of a large garage.

Katie leaned away from Sawyer and grabbed her patchwork clutch purse sitting under the table. She pulled out a pink-and-yellow fabric covered checkbook. Mentally, Katie calculated that her summer camp registrations were due this week, and as long as everyone paid on time, she'd be able to cover all the bills in the next couple days.

Suddenly, Lauren pushed back her chair. "Brownies!" She hopped up and flew across the room toward Gracie, the owner of the River Rock Inn, who exited the small kitchen with a plate of thick chocolate brownies. Gracie stepped toward Lauren on high-heeled red shoes. Her short gingham skirt flared around her toned legs. The sewing circle women often worried about Gracie, as they did about everyone in town. She loved to take long hikes by herself in the surrounding coast mountain range, but she always waved them aside and insisted she was fine and loved the time alone in the woods.

Katie wrote her check and handed it to Beth, who deposited it in a silver money box. She quickly turned and looked into Sawyer's dark eyes. "Don't worry. You know how these things are. People bid on service items and never use them. The money is going to a good cause. That's the important part."

Sawyer's face darkened with emotion. "Glad to help you write that check." Sawyer turned and loped toward the exit.

Katie took a deep breath and tried to calm her racing pulse. She grabbed Lauren's paper and checked Lauren's math, correcting numbers here and there. If only she didn't have to go home and see the lights from Sawyer's mansion glowing across the grassy fields they shared.

Chapter Two

"What are you making, Uncle Sawyer?" Maddie stood on her toes and peered into the blender on the granite kitchen counter. She dipped a spoon into the glass jar and stirred the thick orange liquid.

"It's an energy drink. Carrots. Pineapple. Would you like me to make you one?" Sawyer asked, and smiled at his niece. Six months ago, Maddie and his sister Lisa arrived in Cranberry Bay after Maddie had gotten into trouble with gangs in Seattle. Now, the girl in his kitchen barely resembled the one who had arrived on his doorstep. Seventeen-year-old Maddie's black clothing, dark eyeliner and striped hair had been replaced by a yellow T-shirt and cropped white jeans. Her eyes shone, and she wore a light pink lip gloss. She had pulled her hair back with a silver antique headband that matched the one her mentor, Ivy, had worn at the auction.

Maddie removed the spoon from the jar, wiped her hand on a striped kitchen towel, and reached for one of the gooey cinnamon rolls sitting on a cookie tray on the oven. "These look better." She bit into the roll and chewed while opening the refrigerator and pulling out a carton of orange juice. After pouring herself a large glass, Maddie headed out of the kitchen, passed the large, comfortable green sectional in the family room, and went out the open French doors leading onto the stone patio. She placed her juice on a small table beside a lounge chair and plopped down next to Lisa and Lauren, who both munched on cinnamon rolls. Sawyer loved having his sister and niece living beside him in the carriage house and sharing meals with them.

Sawyer's phone beeped, and he pulled it out of the pocket of his red running shorts. "Auction cleared fifteen-thousand dollars," Josh, who was PTA treasurer, texted.

Sawyer's heart filled. He'd slipped an anonymous envelope filled with hundred-dollar bills into the donation pot and was happy to see the auction's overall total come in so high. The auction provided Cranberry Bay schools with necessities the small town's tax base couldn't afford including: new basketball uniforms for the high school, band equipment for the middle school, and a series of arts-and-crafts enrichment classes for the elementary school. Sawyer had attended Cranberry Bay schools, and he wanted to make sure they could compete with the schools up and down the coast for not only his daughter's generation, but for generations to come.

Sawyer poured the thick carrot juice into a large glass and joined his daughter, sister, and Maddie on the deck. He sat down in a straight-backed chair and eyed the tile work across the back patio. He scanned for small cracks in the grout, his expert eye moving slowly. He enjoyed spending time working on small projects outside the large home. This summer, he planned to put built-in benches around the edges of the fire pit on to the left of the patio as well as a raised garden bed to grow summer veggies.

"Dad." Lauren turned to him with her mouth full of cinnamon roll. "Why can't Maddie live with us in the big house? She could sleep in the room right next to me."

"The carriage house is a great place for Lisa and Maddie," Sawyer said. "Everyone has plenty of space to spread out." He took a long drink of his carrot juice as his good mood faded. He didn't want to tell Lauren the truth. He couldn't bear to open the extra rooms in the house to anyone, not even his sister and niece. The rooms should have been his deceased wife's. Ginger had planned for a sewing room, a library, and their own master suite with a sweeping view of the fields. But she had never lived to see the home finished. When Sawyer completed the home, he closed the upstairs rooms off, choosing to make his own bedroom on the lower level along with his daughter's room. The only person allowed in the upper rooms was his longtime cleaning lady, Karen. Once a month, she quietly went upstairs, dusted, vacuumed, and then shut the empty rooms.

Sawyer stretched his legs in front of him. The morning sun danced in the long grasses, and small birds darted in and out of the flowering pear trees surrounding the home. He had planted the trees because Ginger loved the way the blossoms budded white in the early spring and the tree's purple leaves clung to the limbs until late November, long after every other tree had lost its leaves. As Ginger had struggled to fight the cancer ravaging her body, the trees had given her hope.

Sawyer took another drink of his juice and grimaced. He would have much rather had a Bloody Mary than this concoction.

Lauren and Maddie chattered about the auction the night before, and Lisa leaned over and asked. "How are the AA meetings going?"

"I'm done."

Lisa raised an eyebrow.

"Not really my thing," Sawyer said. "I did what was asked. I stopped drinking. I attended the required AA Meetings for the DUI." He shifted in his chair and lowered his voice, making sure Lauren and Maddie couldn't overhear. "It's a waste of time to sit around in a circle and discuss feelings and life stories."

He didn't need to know every detail of the life stories of people he'd known all his life, and they didn't need to know every detail of his life story. He'd always enjoyed a good Scotch or whiskey to wash the edge off the day, but it seemed that after Ginger died, he couldn't stop at just a couple and would find himself the next morning unsure what had happened the night before. But he had never believed he was an alcoholic. He'd gotten into a bad spot with drinking, and now he'd pulled out of it and had turned things around. He didn't need the meetings. Instead, he'd picked up running, and that seemed to help take away most of the craving. The rest of it, he would tackle the way he had handled everything else, with his own willpower.

"I got it covered," he said.

"Yes." Lisa licked a sticky forefinger. "I guess you've always been good at figuring things out on your own. After Dad died, you took over everything so quickly. I know Mom was relieved to have you helping."

Sawyer nodded. As the oldest of the Shuster clan, it'd been his responsibility to take over the role of being the man in the family after his father died of a sudden heart attack. He knew it was what his father would have expected. At twelve, he took a small job doing odd jobs for a local contractor who had paid him in cash. As he grew older, he took on other jobs with more responsibility and always made sure to give the first part of his check to his mom. It was something he had continued to this day, always making sure she was taken care of as well as his siblings.

"We were always grateful to you." Lisa turned to him and smiled. She uncrossed her legs and tapped his arm. "Even now, you're still taking care of Maddie and me while we try to get our feet on the ground."

"It's what family does." Sawyer picked up his sister's hand and squeezed.

Tears gathered in the corner of Lisa's eyes. Sawyer's heart contracted at seeing his sister in pain. Lisa had not had it easy. Her husband had been killed in a fishing accident in Alaska, and she was left to raise Maddie on her own. Lisa had worked hard at her job as community relations director at a Seattle hospital and built a nice life for herself and Maddie, but she had been forced to give up her job when Maddie got into trouble. The two came home to Cranberry Bay. Lisa had been looking for work for the last six months, but jobs in public relations were coveted and scarce on the coast.

Lisa wiped the corner of her eye and waved her hand over the fields in front of them. "The fields are so pretty in the morning light. Are you still thinking of developing them?"

Sawyer eyed the long grasses shimmering in the light as small birds darted in and out. "I need to get Liberty Bay Square off the ground. It's taking a little more money than I planned." Like many of local developers, he'd gotten stuck with a lot of undeveloped land when the market crashed. It'd taken a few years, but things were slowly coming back to life.

"But you are still planning the development?" Lisa pressed him.

"Yes." Sawyer nodded. When he had bought the property, he had intended to build his house and then subdivide the property into small lots where homeowners could share common areas and gardens. But after the fight with the council and town over the homes on the hillside, he had stepped back for a while to allow the dust to settle. He knew it wasn't profitable, but a part of him enjoyed the empty fields and didn't want to see all of the land developed.

"The barn is beautiful in the morning," Lisa said. "The light bounces off the wood and gives it such a glimmer."

"You're not going to tear down the barn?" Maddie asked, nodding to the large wooden building on the edge of the field.

"No." Sawyer shifted, aware that Maddie and Lauren had stopped talking and been listening to their conversation. He gazed over the fields to the run-down building and stiffened. "The structure belongs to Katie."

When he purchased twenty acres of the former dairy's farmland, he had intended to buy the barn and tear it down.

But Katie had stepped in and persuaded her uncle not to sell it to him. It was a poor move as far as he was concerned as it meant as an acre of his property ran between her home and the barn, but she hadn't budged.

"You don't like Katie?" Maddie asked.

"She doesn't understand business." Sawyer wanted to be careful about what he said in front of Lauren. Lauren adored Katie, and he had to admit, although he and Katie fought on opposite sides of town issues, the relationship between his daughter and Katie had eased some of Lauren's grief over losing her mother.

Maddie's eyes widened. "But she runs the New Leaf Sewing Shop and is president of the Small Business Association. Everyone loves Katie."

Sawyer bit back the words on the tip of his tongue. Everyone loved Katie but him.

"It was the conference center." Lisa shook her head at her daughter. "There was a little problem with a conference center a few years ago."

"What happened?" Maddie leaned forward, her eyes big and bright.

Sawyer grimaced. "I was trying to bring business to Cranberry Bay. A conference center would have meant increased business for all of the small shops. But she started a Cranberry Bay Friends Group and fought me at every turn. They delayed the permit process for so long that the center finally pulled out and went to Seaview Point."

It had been his only loss as a developer, and even thinking about it made him churn. Katie never understood that to keep the small town alive, they had to keep moving forward in their goals and developments. Sawyer stared into the fields. Her aunt and uncle had understood when they sold him the land from their dairy farm. They understood that to have their dream of retiring in Florida, they had to sell the unused dairy farm. But Katie wanted to block progress, namely his, at every turn.

Every time he turned around, Katie showed up and infuriated him. Last night's auction was only another example. He knew his reputation in the town had been tarnished in the last couple years because of the slope-property-development fight, which had dragged on for over a year, but to have Katie buy his services out of pity sent his blood boiling. He did not need or want anyone's pity and, most of all, not Katie's.

"Dad!" Lauren placed her hands on her hips of her denim overalls. "You weren't listening."

"I was listening." Sawyer shifted to face her. At times, he saw the reflection of his late wife in his daughter, and the feeling both comforted and made him ache with an untold longing.

Lisa buried her smile in a big sip of coffee.

Maddie nodded her head in agreement with Lauren. "You weren't listening. You were staring at that barn like you wanted to demolish it with your hands."

Sawyer grinned at Maddie's honesty. Maddie was right. He had let his emotions control him. He hated allowing his emotions to get the best of him. It'd been much easier to control feelings when he drank. He numbed everything out with another drink. When he wasn't drinking, he was too busy dealing with the aftereffects to feel anything.

"Sorry." He turned to his daughter while hoping to change the conversation. "So what's on your agenda this morning?"

"I want to ride my bike." Lauren's hands stayed on her hips. "And I can't ride on the gravel driveway. Remember what happened last time?"

Sawyer nodded. He didn't need any reminders of her sharp piercing screams as she tried to ride her bike on the gravel and ended up with small pebbles embedded into her knees.

"Can you take me to Grandma's house? She has all the sidewalks."

"Of course." Sawyer turned on his phone and flipped to his calendar. He scrolled through his daily notes, noting what details he needed to work out for Liberty Bay Square. He still had at least one empty storefront, and he wished a bike shop had taken him up on his offer to move into the new shopping area. The whole town had gone bike-crazy this summer. He wasn't sure what started it, but everyone suddenly had a bike. Biking had always been great in the upper streets of Cranberry Bay along the sidewalks stretching beside the two-story Craftsman homes where he'd grown up. Sawyer scrolled through the notes, and, seeing a block of time in the afternoon said, "How about you and I go ride our bikes together later this afternoon?"

"You know how to ride a bike?" Lauren eyed him.

Lisa burst out laughing. "Your Dad used to ride his bike all over Cranberry Bay."

Lauren continued to study him like a math problems she couldn't figure out.

"I know how to ride." Sawyer rubbed his neck. "I just need to get stretched out a bit." He grimaced. His morning workouts pushed muscles that hadn't been used in years. He'd always loved running and often enjoyed jogging along the rural roads surrounding his large home. But while he was drinking, it seemed to take all his energy just to keep his job going. Mornings became more about managing the night before, and by the time he felt like doing anything, the thought of a beer sounded better than a jog. Eventually, it would feel good to do those morning runs again.

Lauren danced off the porch. "I'll get my bike!"

Maddie grinned and scurried off the chaise lounge. "I'll see if she needs any help. I might have to get a bike myself this summer. I bet Ivy could help me find a really great vintage bike."

Lisa took another sip of coffee as the girls ran off together. "I remember you and Ginger used to ride all over Cranberry Bay. I always wanted to come with you, but you said I wasn't invited."

"I remember." Sawyer said, his voice dark and heavy as the familiar twinge of pain filled his chest. Ginger had been his high school sweetheart. He had promised to protect and love her for the rest of his life. He had believed he needed to be a good provider, and he'd spent hours and hours away from her, building his business. When he did come home, they argued about everything, and he escaped to the garage to soothe himself with drink after drink. He believed they could work it out, but before he had a chance to show her how much he loved her, she'd gotten ovarian cancer and slipped away from him. Unable to bear losing her, he'd increased his drinking, using anything to numb the pain of knowing that he had failed and lost the only woman he'd ever loved.

"It wasn't your fault," Lisa said and touched his arm.

Sawyer looked away from his sister. It was his fault. He had failed Ginger. He had proven he was unable to protect her. He vowed to never fail anyone again, and the best way to do that was simply to never fall in love again.

Chapter Three

Katie shifted on the stool at the counter of the fabric shop and scanned the pattern order form for summer camp. A pink candle glowed by her side and filled the room with ambrosia. A light rain tapped on the sidewalks and into the hanging baskets, which hung from the eaves along Main Street. Tiny starts of red geraniums, crystal blue lobelia, and white petunias whispered of colorful flowers, which would spill over the basket's edges by July. In the back of the room, sewing machines hummed as Ivy and Rylee worked on the sewing circle's latest project, festive summer beach bags.

The bell above the shop door chimed, and Sasha, bakery owner and sewing circle member, stumbled inside with her hands full of fabric. She dumped various triangle shapes on the counter and slumped against it. "Help." Sasha ran her hand across her forehead as lines tightened over her narrow face. Her ponytail stuck out the back end of a purple baseball cap and matched the purple sweatshirt she wore over faded blue jeans. "I've made a big mess."

Katie picked up an odd-shaped triangle of canvas fabric. "What is this supposed to be?"

"Tyler is playing in the baseball tournament, and I'm on the decorating committee. It's supposed to be a flag for each team. We're going to hang the banners from the top of the bleachers."

"It looks like the measurements on the canvas aren't quite right. When is the tournament?" Katie loved helping solve the sewing problems of Cranberry Bay. The New Leaf Sewing Shop had originally been a scrapbook shop run by her mom. As a teenager, Katie spent many afternoons and weekends working the cash register. Women brought pictures of family picnics, weddings, and birthdays, and, as they picked colors for pages, they shared their joys and sorrows. Even when her mom was undergoing cancer treatments, she never tired of taking the time to problem-solve not only the layout of a scrapbook page but also life's problems. After her mother died and she inherited the small shop, Katie had changed to selling fabric but pledged to continue the tradition of being a place of community for people of all ages to share their joys and sorrows. She held meetings for the Friends of Cranberry Bay at the back table, hosted small groups of women who wanted to learn to sew everything from vintage bridal veils to elaborate scarves, and acted as the Small Business Association's place to find solace and comfort during the long rainy winter days when customers were far and few between. Life on Main Street revolved around the New Leaf Sewing Shop, and Katie wouldn't have had it any other way.

"The tournament is the July Fourth weekend." Sasha brushed a large patch of flour from her pant leg and lowered her voice. "I wasn't going to enter Tyler in the games. It's too much money for the full weekend. But his coach really wants him to participate. He says Tyler has a good arm, and he thinks it might be something to develop for high school." Sasha shook her head, and her voice saddened. "It must be his dad's influence."

Katie nodded. She knew better than to bring any more pain to Sasha by talking about Tyler's dad. "The tournament is six weeks away." Katie eyed Sasha. "You have plenty of time to figure out the flags."

"I've got too much to do at the bakery." Sasha slumped against the counter. Dark circles lined her eyes.

"Do you have a large order between now and then?" The bakery, two stores down from the sewing shop, often shone with lights late at night or early in the morning as Sasha worked steadily to keep her business going. Although she hired a couple of high school girls to help her with the counter, the baking all fell on Sasha's shoulders.

"Just a friendly small town pie competition." Sasha straightened and grinned.

"Pie competition?" Ivy asked as she clipped corners of a red, white, and blue fabric at a large table in the back of the room.

Sasha headed to the back of the room. She pulled out a chair opposite Ivy and sunk into it. "Beth thinks her pies are the best in town, and those are the only ones we should serve at the baseball tournament." She rolled her eyes. "I challenged her to a pie bake-off competition, and we're going to let the town decide whose pies get sold at the games."

"That's a great idea." Rylee stuck blue-and-white star fabric under the needle of her sewing machine. "We could set a couple of ballot boxes and pies at Bryan's office." She winked. "I'm sure he can help influence the vote."

"Great idea," Katie said as the door to the shop swung open along with a large gust of rain. Lauren danced inside. She waved a yellow flier in the air. "I want to sign up for summer sewing camp." She shook water from her yellow rain jacket as she jerked off her hood.

"Which session would you like? We have three." Katie gave Lauren a hug and reached to the wall behind the counter for her clipboard of upcoming camp sessions. Each session still had one or two slots open, so Lauren could have her pick. But even if the sessions had filled, Katie would still have found room for her favorite sewer.

Katie turned around with the clipboard as Sawyer closed the door behind him. She inhaled sharply. He wore a dark rain jacket over his T-shirt and had unzipped it to reveal a white dress shirt over black slacks. Sawyer's gaze met hers, and for an instant something sparked between them. Katie returned her focus to Lauren but not before heat rose in her cheeks.

"I want to be in all of the sessions." Lauren skipped to the large table and leaned over Rylee's shoulder. "I want to learn to sew everything."

"Lauren, we talked about this," Sawyer said, his voice calm and steady. "I thought you wanted to take one of the hiking camps with Adam."

Katie smiled. Youngest Shuster brother, Adam, lived and breathed the outdoors. His summer hiking camps always filled with kids from all over the state.

"I love Uncle Adam. But I want to sew with Katie." Lauren placed her hands on her hips. "I want to be in the sewing circle like Aunt Rylee."

"I'm just Rylee," Rylee said, and smiled. "Not Aunt Rylee."

"But you will be my aunt," Lauren whirled to face a pink-cheeked Rylee. "You and Bryan are getting married." She drew out the word married and twirled in a circle. "Maybe I can even be the flower girl."

"Lauren," Sawyer said. "Let's not jump ahead of ourselves."

"It's okay," Rylee said. "I'll check with Bryan, but we'd love to have you be our flower girl."

"Tyler wants to attend to sewing camp, too." Sasha sorted her pile of canvas and tossed aside another odd-shaped banner. "He wants to learn how to sew denim tool belts for his new hobby of fixing everything around the bakery. Maybe I should let him make these banners." She frowned at the crumpled fabric in front of her.

"I want to be with Tyler." Lauren skated to Sasha's chair. "Can you sign him up for the same camp as me?"

Sasha raised an eyebrow and looked above Lauren's head to Katie.

"Of course." Katie jotted Tyler's name beside Lauren's. It was hard to not enjoy watching the budding friendship between Tyler and Lauren. The little girl seemed to struggle to make friends with the other girls in her class, and Katie wasn't sure why. She'd tried to talk to Lauren about having some of her friends over to make cookies, but Lauren always dodged the invitation and changed the subject. Katie didn't want to pry, but she worried about Lauren.

"Excuse me." Sawyer yanked his phone out of his pocket and frowned. He reached up and adjusted his earpiece and strode toward a tall shelf of pastel cotton fabrics. He lowered his voice as he spoke into his Bluetooth.

Katie beckoned to Lauren. "Let's pick out your fabric for your first pillowcase project. We'll need a primary fabric and a contrasting one." She loved teaching the young people of Cranberry Bay how to sew. She had spent many hours learning to sew with her mother. They had often scrounged thrift stores searching for jeans, skirts, and tops that could be refitted. They'd made a game out of it, disguising the fact that they couldn't afford to buy new clothing. If Katie suspected an article of clothing might be recognized by its previous owner, she sewed on embroidered hearts and swirls across jeans legs and collars, which gave everything a new look. By the time Katie was a teenager, she sewed all of her clothing and was often asked to sew dresses for formal school dances of her classmates. She loved all of it and still took consignment sewing jobs when people needed special dresses for weddings and dances.

Lauren headed to the summer beach-themed fabrics. "Your fabric is so much better than Craft Mart." She yanked the bolt off the shelf, and two others tumbled beside it. Lauren wrinkled her nose. "Craft Mart never has any fun things like beach fabric. I'm always going to shop at your store."

Katie leaned over to pick up one of the bolts. "We don't have to worry about which store you'll shop at because the nearest Craft Mart is in Portland." Katie clamped her lips tight as a jolt of fear shot through her chest. She licked her lips, which had suddenly gone dry. She hoped the nearest store was in Portland. Sawyer had promised the large stores of Liberty Bay Square would not threaten any of the Main Street shops. But no one trusted Sawyer, least of all her.

During the last few weeks, he had slipped an office supply store into the Liberty Bay Square roster and insisted it would not compete with Dave Ward's family owned pharmacy, which stocked office supplies. Sawyer said the large chain office store would draw people who wanted items ranging from discounted printer ink to paper for both small-business and home use. Dave had been devastated and spent hours talking to Katie. Katie, as well as the other owners in the Small Business Association, vowed never to step foot in the office supply shop at Liberty Bay Square. Each promised Dave he could still count on their orders for sales receipts, ink, and pens.

Katie sorted through bolts of fabric with Lauren as Rylee, Sasha, and Ivy chattered about the upcoming baseball tournament. She made a mental note to check with the city Planning Commission on the final list of Sawyer's stores, just in case something had changed in the last few weeks.

"If the baseball tournament is on the Fourth of July, they won't let us host the vintage market at the school. The teams will be using the locker rooms and be in and out of the gym." Rylee removed her fabric from the machine. She ran her finger down the seam and moved to the ironing board.

"What about your barn, Katie?" Ivy cut a narrow strip of red, white, and blue fabric. Her half-sewn summer beach bag lay across the table.

"My barn?" Katie straightened a bolt of fabric with blue stars. She couldn't imagine using her barn for a public event.

It'd never pass inspection, and they didn't have a lot of time to get the necessary permits from the city.

"The barn would be a great place to have the market." Sasha stood and headed for a bolt of canvas fabric. She yanked it from the shelf and walked to the cutting table. "We could have vendors who needed more space for large items set up outside with covered awnings in case it rained."

"But the location is too far away from the town. How will people find us?" Katie shook her head as Lauren pulled out the bolt of beach ball fabric that matched Rylee's bag.

"It's not that far out of town." Ivy sat down at one of the machines and threaded it with white thread. "We could set up a few sandwich board signs."

"But the building needs a lot of work." Katie continued to protest as she rearranged a display of summer bag patterns on a spinning rack. "I don't think we'd even pass inspection at this point. We only have six weeks before the July Fourth weekend."

It wasn't just hosting the event in the barn. It was something more. Something that tugged at a deep part of her she kept hidden. If they opened the barn to the public, she was exposing herself and where she lived. It was one thing to have people come to the shop, but to open the place she called home to the public? Katie's stomach shivered. She stopped and took a deep breath, reminding herself she had nothing to hide. She was no longer a child concealing her father's abuse and afraid to allow people to come to her home.

Sawyer stepped from behind the back shelf and pocketed his phone. "What needs a lot of work?"

"My barn." Katie tightened her lips. Why did it seem Sawyer always stepped in at the worst possible time?

"Dad could help you!" Lauren said.

Katie tried to smile at Lauren. After all, she had bid on her father's handyman services at the auction. She didn't want to tell her she never planned to use them. That would only hurt the little girl, and her whole purpose for buying the services had been so Lauren would not hurt.

"Lauren is correct. My handyman services could do the work for you." Sawyer leaned against the counter and crossed his arms across his chest. He studied Katie with a glint in his dark eyes. "The services you bought at the auction."

Katie steeled her shoulders. "I am aware of what services I own." The man could infuriate her and raise the heat to her cheeks faster than anyone she knew.

Sawyer nodded, and his eyes never left her face. Katie's toes curled as his eyes held hers. Why did she have to feel such an attraction to this man who was her foe so often?

"We can't cancel the market," Ivy said. "The vendors have already confirmed with Lisa. We need a large space to hold everyone."

Katie's stomach muscles clenched. They only had a few weeks before Lisa needed to prepare the marketing materials. She had already set up a Facebook page for the market as well as other social media accounts to build anticipation. Katie shifted away from Sawyer and eyed the hopeful faces of her friends. She couldn't let everyone down because she didn't want to work with Sawyer. She had never let her personal resentment stand in the way of building community, and she wouldn't start now.

"Yes." Katie turned back to Sawyer, making sure to keep her voice even as she forced herself to remain steady. "I would like to use the certificate from the auction for your services."

"I'll come by and take a look at the barn. I can let you know how much work will need to be done to get it up to code." Sawyer pulled out his phone and punched in a quick note to himself. He pocketed his phone, and as his dark eyes met Katie's, small flutters filled her chest against her will.

She held herself firmly and met his eyes. "Thank you." The words sounded pleasant and did not betray her beating heart. How would she ever be able to spend days with Sawyer working on the barn and not fall into the attraction bubbling between them?

Chapter Four

The sound of children playing tag carried on the afternoon breeze across to the park as the warm sun poured across Sawyer's back. He pounded another nail into the summer music stage's floorboard. The makeshift stage had been placed on the hillside above the river, which rushed with water from heavy spring rains and mountain snowmelt. A few feet away, a metal rack of tire tubes sat beside a hut with brown shingles. A small sign hung outside. "Closed for the Season." It'd be weeks before the river was low enough for anyone to go tubing without the risk of being tossed into the cold water and thrown onto the rocks.

"How about we set this up by the covered picnic area?" Bryan pointed to a metal bike rack. He eyes peered from under his baseball cap, and with his cutoff jeans and white T-shirt dotted with redwood stain splotches, no one would have recognized him as the north coast's most successful real estate agent for the last quarter. An honor Bryan attributed to his new passion for life, thanks to his engagement with Rylee.

"Great idea." The youngest Shuster brother, Adam, lifted one end of the bike rack as Bryan hefted the other. They moved the metal structure to an enclosed area with picnic tables and a barbecue. Adam's khaki shorts were covered with dirt. He'd spent the morning digging out a space for the new bike pathway, which followed along the edges of the park and connected to the paved river trail running to the edges of town. Adam had been one of the early supporters of the bikes and worked tirelessly to create new paths all over town.

Sawyer enjoyed working with his brothers to ready the park for the summer concert series. Their parents had always supported the town's art programs and helped bring the concert series to town when the boys were small children. The boys grew up listening to everything from jazz to rock to big band. They enjoyed summer nights in the park with their mom's thick BLT sandwiches, pink lemonade, and signature chocolate brownies.

Every spring, Dad and three of his closest friends constructed the summer concert stage. After Dad died, Dad's friends continued building the stage until Adam took the Parks and Recreation Department job. He had immediately enlisted the volunteer help of Sawyer and Bryan. The older men still enjoyed coming out to spend time in the park and offer advice, but they usually spent their time on the benches and allowed the three Shuster boys to do most of the work.

"There is a lot of excitement about the sporting goods store at Liberty Bay Square," Adam said. "The folks at Parks and Recreation are happy not to have to drive to Portland for new hiking gear."

"We've needed a sporting goods store for a long time." Bryan lowered his voice. "Tom tries to bring in some gear to his hardware shop, but it's just not the same as we can get at the sporting goods shops in Portland. Are all the leases signed?"

"Everyone but one." Sawyer's voice darkened.

"Which one?" Bryan asked.

"The end anchor store."

Adam whistled. "You don't have an anchor store lease? Isn't that a little bit of a problem?"

Sawyer hardened his voice. The last remaining store had been a sore spot for weeks. He had hoped to have it worked out long before now. "I wanted to secure a lease with a large pet shop that has grooming, too. I thought it'd really be a hit with the beach folks. But it hasn't gone as planned." Sawyer grimaced.

"Beach towns have the pet market cornered." Adam shook his head. "People want to shop the small stores located on Main Streets by the beach. They pick up last-minute doggie beach toys and treats. It's hard to compete with the free treats dogs get as soon as they step paw in the shops." He chuckled.

Sawyer ran his hand through his hair. "It's not just the local shops. The groomers aren't too happy. It seems a group of the groomers got together and wrote a few nasty reviews about dogs getting bad cuts at the major chain. Nothing sends people scurrying for the hills like Fido going to come home with a bad haircut."

A tennis ball landed at Sawyer's feet. He picked it up and tossed the ball back to Tom Hathaway and his springer spaniel, Brittany. Tom, owner of the town hardware store, had been bringing Brittany to work with him for the last twelve years. Every day at lunch, the two played catch in the park, rain or shine.

"We need to get the local groomers on board," Bryan said. "Dogs like Brittany need a place to go get a new collar or leash. The closest pet shop is at the beach, twenty miles away."

"Too late," Sawyer said. "The pet store just pulled out last night."

"What other stores are you considering?" Adam asked. "There have to be some other good ones that want to come to Cranberry Bay."

"Craft Mart," Sawyer said. "They think our market would be perfect for them. Everyone wants to take those shells they find at the beach and make necklaces and glue them on frames. I'm going to send some paperwork over to them this afternoon."

Bryan shook his head and nodded to the New Leaf Sewing Shop. "I think you might get a fight on that one."

"Craft Mart sells craft supplies, not just fabric. Everyone will still shop at her store. She knows how to handle herself. It's business. Katie is a businesswoman." Sawyer pounded the nail into the wooden board as the door to Katie's shop opened, and she stepped outside. She lifted a watering can to the hanging baskets. Drops fell out of the heavy baskets and onto the sidewalk. Sawyer couldn't take his gaze off her long legs extending from under a short peach skirt. Her thick hair danced around her shoulders and fell across a cream blouse. What would it be like to hold her in his arms and dance in the starlit summer sky while the music played softly around them? He imagined running his hands through her thick gorgeous hair and inhaling her soft scent.

Suddenly, as if she heard his thoughts, Katie turned and gazed at him. Her eyes met his, and her face softened. Without thinking about it, Sawyer lifted his left hand in a small wave and then stiffened as a white box truck sped past on Main Street. A small group of kids whizzed by on bikes along the sidewalk. A dark-haired girl, who looked to be about Lauren's age, trailed behind the cluster of kids. Sawyer didn't recognize her as anyone in Lauren's small class and figured she was a friend of someone, visiting from one of the beach towns. The girl worked to keep her bike steady but swerved dangerously close to the street.

Sawyer stood. It wasn't safe to have large trucks speeding down Main Street and bikers on the narrow, uneven sidewalk. He made a note to talk to Jason Steidel, chief of police, about getting some traffic revisions or a lowered speed limit put in place, at least for the summer when the bike traffic would be the heaviest.

Sawyer glanced back across the street, hoping to see Katie still looking at him. Instead, she had moved to talk to the dark-haired girl, who stopped her bike outside Sasha's bakery. Sawyer found his heart dropping because Katie wasn't looking at him. He shook his head. Where had that thought come from? The last person he ever wanted to entertain romantic thoughts about or to be the focus of her romantic thoughts was Katie.

Bryan wiped his hands on his shorts. "I'm ready for a cool one on the deck. Sawyer, you coming with us?"

"Not for me." Sawyer shook his head. "I'm going to head out for a run." He missed a good beer after a hard day's work, but he couldn't chance it. One drink, and he'd be back down the drinking path. He'd head out for a run and shake off the feelings about Katie that continued to cling to him.

***

An hour later, Sawyer slowed his jogging pace to a walk and headed toward his house. It'd been a good five-mile run on the lightly traveled rural roads. He stopped short at the edge of his property. A dented camper trailer was parked sideways across the field. The peaceful feeling of his run faded, and Sawyer swore under his breath. He lived just far enough off the main highway that people often left old pieces of furniture and mattresses on his property. The worst were the stray cats and dogs that made their way to his back porch. He tried to keep most of them from Lauren, but sometimes she found a kitten or nine-month-old malnourished dog first. Together, they'd feed the animal and pack it into the car and drive it over to the county animal rescue. Each trip resulted in Lauren's cries and pleadings to keep the animals. And each time, Sawyer's heart ached as he had to tell his daughter no. They couldn't keep all of the animals.

Sawyer steeled his shoulders and headed toward the dingy white thirteen-foot camper. It was too late in the day, and the junkyard would be closed. But tomorrow, he'd hook it up to his truck and haul it out bright and early. He needed to get a good look at the hitch and make sure it could be hauled.

As he approached the camper, Katie stepped out the door. She carried a clipboard in her hand, and her hair was pulled up in a ponytail that stuck out the back of a baseball cap. She had changed from her peach skirt and white blouse into a pair of tight denim shorts and an old T-shirt that outlined every curve. He had a hard time taking his eyes off of her, and all the running he had just done to push her out of his mind hadn't completely submerged his emotions. They surged back into him with a force that took his breath away.

"Someone left this?" Sawyer asked. He hoped his voice sounded steady.

"No." Katie scanned his running shorts and tank top before lifting her eyes to his face. "It belongs to me. Ivy helped me move it out of the barn with her truck."

"It's a 1971 Trailblazer," Sawyer said.

"Yes," Katie's eyes widened in surprise. "It belonged to my mom and I. We lived in it for a year." Her voice broke off and she tightened her lips.

"How about we move it off my property? I bet there are other places it could go." Sawyer motioned to the barn. He sensed the pain under Katie's words but didn't want to push. His main goal was to get the camper off his property.

"The camper is not on your property. It's on my property."

"I'm pretty sure this part of the land belongs to me." Sawyer waved at the strip of land between the barn and Katie's home. "This is the acre that belongs to me, but your barn sits on it." Sawyer walked up to the side and ran his hands over the paint-chipped panel of the Trailblazer. The smell of dead mice drifted out the open windows. Sawyer fought not to cover his nose with his hand. "What are you planning to do with it? Surely not take this out camping?" He pressed his hand against a wheel, and it squished under his fingers. "I think you've got at least one bad wheel if not a whole set."

"I'm going to rehab it." Katie's face lightened. "I'm going to use it for the vintage market and have some of my special fabrics and notions for sale."

"Well, it needs to be moved." Sawyer ran his hand over the hitch. It looked strong enough for a trip to the side of the barn. "I'll grab my truck, and we'll get it hooked up. Be right back."

Sawyer jogged across the field to his driveway. He hopped inside and, in seconds, pulled up in front of the camper. He hitched the trailer to the back and headed toward the barn. The rain had worn away the gravel and turned it into large sinkholes. Sawyer glanced at the small one-story ranch house. The cheery curtains at the windows gave the home a feeling of comfort and warmth. But eyeballing the peeling paint on the exterior, he realized the soft touches masked a home in need of some work.

Sawyer pulled up alongside the barn. Shingles dripped off the edges. Large pieces of wood hung at angles along the back wall. The large doors stood ajar and crooked. Sawyer rubbed his eyes. He had agreed to the handyman job, and he wouldn't back out, but it was going to take a lot of work to get the barn up to code in time for the market. "I need some help watching the mirrors to back up the trailer." Sawyer leaned over and opened the passenger door.

Katie slid inside, and the smell of honeysuckle and lavender sent him reeling. Sawyer's hands froze to the steering wheel as something inside him had woken up, as if from a long nap. He pressed down on the gas harder than he intended, and the camper slammed against the barn. A few of the shingles fell off the roof as the barn shook.

Sawyer clenched his jaw, turned off the truck, and stepped out. He leaned over and picked up a broken shingle. "I think you need a new roof."

Katie crossed her arms over her chest and bit down on her lower lip. "I'm sure that's not part of your handyman services."

Sawyer shook his head. The last thing he wanted to do was put a new roof on the barn. He had hoped the job would be a small one, and he could be on his way. But something else gnawed at him. He needed his Liberty Bay Square stores to succeed. His future developments hinged on this one. He needed people to attend the opening weekend, and the way to do that was to prove to the people of Cranberry Bay he could be trusted. His developments brought work to the town. But no one seemed to understand. Sawyer tapped his foot. The way to get people to see him differently was to start with Katie. She was one of the town's leaders. People loved her. If she spoke highly of him, people would begin to trust in his vision for the town and what he could do as a developer.

"I'll be by in the morning to get started. I can whip the roof out in a few days or so." Sawyer stepped into his truck. He rolled down the window. "I know we sit on opposite sides of the fence in this town. But on this job, we are a team."

Sawyer turned and backed down the driveway. And something inside him lightened.

Chapter Five

Katie shuffled the camp registrations and set them on the back table beside each machine. She double-checked to make sure each of the places had a package of gray thread, bobbin, scissors, and detailed pillowcase handout. Satisfied everything was ready for the first session of summer camp, Katie rubbed the aching muscles in her forearms. She had ridden her bike to the shop the last couple of mornings. If she left early, she could bike the rural roads without worrying about running into any traffic. After work, the eight o'clock sunset made for perfect summer evenings for taking bike rides on the river trail and dodging what seemed like the entire town who'd gone bike crazy as they sped by her on everything from ten-speed bikes to old-fashioned one-speeds. She pushed aside the small voice that whispered that her new hours avoided Sawyer working on the barn and had nothing to do with riding a bike to work.

"Mm ..." Tyler leaned against the front counter and took another bite of berry cobbler. A small sliver of red berries ran down his cheeks. His blond hair fell forward into his blue eyes. He wore a faded sweatshirt with the elementary school's eagle mascot. His too-long sleeves hit the counter as he forked pieces of the pie.

"What do you think?" Sasha wiped the berries off her son's face. She tapped her fingers on the counter and shuffled her feet, encased in her worn and dependable clogs.

"I don't know." Tyler shoveled in another large bite of pie. He eyed the blueberry pie sitting on the counter. "I might have to try that one too."

"You can try all of them." Sasha brushed a lock of hair away from her son's forehead. "Just as long as you tell all your friend's parents to vote for my pies." Her voice took on a determined tone.

"I'll try a piece of that pie." Katie didn't tell Sasha, but she had left a piece of strawberry pie on a paper plate in the backroom. Beth had brought her pie earlier that morning in the hopes that a recommendation from Katie would ensure votes from many of the downtown shop owners. Katie had politely thanked Beth while knowing her loyalty to Sasha ensured Sasha received her vote. Even if the pie were terrible, she'd never betray her friend by voting for Beth.

A loud clatter of metal rose outside the open door as Lauren, Emma, and Morgan's bikes crashed together in a heap. Katie made a quick note to herself that she needed to get a bike rack like the other shops. She tucked her own bike in the backroom, but she'd never be able to store all the bikes in the small storeroom.

"I'll take care of the bikes," Sasha said. "I've got to get back to the bakery and check on the orders for tomorrow. I'll see you in a few hours to pick up Tyler." Sasha nodded to Katie as Morgan and Emma burst through the door, and Lauren lagged behind them. Morgan and Emma wore matching crop jean shorts with sparkling hearts lining the cuffs. Their light green T-shirts matched the beaded necklaces and earrings they each wore. Both girls linked arms as they giggled and strolled through the fabric aisles to the back of the room.

Lauren trailed behind them and wandered down an aisle on the edge of the store, her eyes downcast and her feet moving heavily on the linoleum.

Katie frowned as Morgan touched her on the arm. She broke away from Emma and stepped closer to Katie. "My mom forgot to give me money," Morgan whispered, and her face flushed. "I haven't picked out any fabric."

"I've got it covered and will talk to your mom." Morgan's family lived on her father's disability checks. They didn't have money for extra activities like sewing camp, and Morgan had been enrolled with one of the scholarships Katie had donated at the auction and Emma's mom had bought.

"Thank you." Morgan linked her arm back with Emma's, and the two headed into the pink fabric collection.

Katie nodded. She remembered her own childhood days of going into a large craft store and believing she could buy a set of new watercolors and paper. Her mom showed her the coupon and said it was for her birthday. But when they arrived at the counter, the clerk insisted the coupon was not valid for the brand she'd chosen. The coupon brand had sold out. The clerk would not offer a discount, and her mom hadn't enough money to complete the purchase. Mortified, Katie left the supplies on the counter and slipped out of the store. She had vowed never to allow the same thing to happen in her business.

Lauren slunk into one of the plastic school chairs set at the back table. She placed her elbows on the table and dropped her head into her hands.

"What's wrong?" Katie sat down beside Lauren. She often had to work a young sewer through their frustrations and believed it was best to sit eye to eye.

"Nothing." Lauren shook her head. She eyed Morgan and Katie, who had both pulled pre-cut yards of matching fabric and sat down side-by-side at the other end of the table. The girls leaned their heads together and chattered without looking up at Lauren.

"I have a piece of pie in the backroom," Katie whispered. "Beth brought it by, but I didn't want to hurt Sasha's feelings. Would you like it?"

Lauren shook her head as Tyler pulled out a chair and plunked down beside her. He dropped his folded fabric in front of her. "Look what I picked out. Whatcha got for your pillowcase? Something girly?"

Lauren's face lightened. "I don't have something girly." She reached into her backpack and pulled out a yard of pink shell fabric.

Katie stared at the fabric. She didn't have to look hard to know it wasn't a brand she carried. Craft Mart carried the brand.

"I thought you were going to use the beach ball fabric like Rylee's," Katie said, making sure to keep her voice light. Why was Lauren using fabric carried by Craft Mart instead of the fabric she sold? She didn't require the campers to buy fabric from her, and some of them did come with material that had been stuffed in attics and closets, but Lauren had specifically chosen fabric from her store. Had Sawyer and Lauren made a trip to Craft Mart in Portland to buy fabric? It seemed like a far stretch to her, but maybe they had taken a day to do some shopping and stopped by the superstore.

"Dad gave me this," Lauren said. "It's okay to use?" She frowned.

Katie's stomach plummeted. Sawyer had given her the fabric. They hadn't gone shopping for it. Did Sawyer have fabric from Craft Mart because sales representatives had talked to Sawyer about opening a store and left samples of products for him to give out to tempt future customers?

"Of course," Katie rubbed Lauren's shoulders and pushed away her fears. "I was just surprised." She did not want Lauren to see she was upset. It didn't matter what fabric Lauren used for the project. The important thing was for Lauren to be happy with her finished pillowcase.

But as soon as she could, she was going to ask Sawyer about Lauren's fabric choice.

***

The evening sun slipped below the horizon as Katie adjusted the small blue face mask over her nose and the smell of dead mice crept inside. She chewed hard on her spearmint gum and bit back the urge to throw up. She'd worked hard searching and removing every dead mouse she could find tucked into the cabinets and crevices of the old trailer. But she still hadn't located the last one.

Ivy poked her head into the trailer's open door. "Hello. Anyone here?"

Katie lifted her arm to motion Ivy inside. Every muscle in her body ached. She moved her fingers inside the heavy-duty work gloves and tried to steel herself to finish the job. The first bench seat next to the table had come out easily. She had unscrewed a few bolts, and the seat slipped right out. But the second one remained in place by the window and wouldn't budge. She might have left it in place, but the last dead mouse had to be behind the seat. The torn cushion looked like it'd been a nice home for a family of rodents.

"What a project!" Ivy stepped around bench seats and a small table, which lay on their sides. A torn seat cushion was piled on top of the ripped green awning.

Katie nodded. The trailer had turned into more of a project then she'd anticipated. As a teenager, she'd learned how to fix everything from adding new caulking in the bathroom tiles to fixing the garage disposal in the kitchen. She enjoyed fixing things. It seemed easier to learn to replace a broken tile than to fix the tension in the house. Her aunt and uncle had not wanted them living in the home and always complained of the extra expenses, even though Katie's mom did her best with her contributions from the scrapbook store.

Ivy fingered a swatch of red-and-white gingham plaid fabric. "Are you using this for the curtains?"

"Curtains and new matching seat cushions," Katie said, her heart lifting at what would be the next stage of refurnishing the old camper.

Ivy dropped a piece of paper on the torn linoleum counter. "Sawyer's on the agenda for the council again."

"What is it this time?" Katie pushed back a strand of hair from her eyes while, at the same time, her stomach dove into her feet.

"Liberty Bay Square." Ivy lowered her voice. "Sawyer has added a new store to his list."

"Craft Mart." Katie barely breathed the words. She knew it. She had known it as soon as she'd seen the fabric Lauren had for camp. Sawyer was bringing Craft Mart to Cranberry Bay, and it would threaten everything she held dear in the store she inherited from her mom.

Ivy grimaced. "The pet store fell through, and Craft Mart was waiting to get into our market. There's some issue with Craft Mart's plans for a fireworks show on the opening day, and he needs to get the city's approval for a special permit."

Craft Mart with their discount coupons and huge sales every week. Craft Mart with their cheap fabric that they sold at deeply discounted prices. Katie could barely breathe. Her pulse raced.

"Maybe he can be swayed to find a different store," Ivy said. "There have to be others. A clothing store? A discount furniture store? Something?"

"No. If he's asking for approval for a fireworks show, they've signed the lease." Katie shook her head as a yellow striped cat wound its way around her legs. She loved the barn cats. Most remained outdoors, but a few found their way into the house. A black-and-white tuxedo cat spent its days sleeping on her bed, and a tabby preferred the living room couch to the scratchy hay in the barn. Last summer, a gray-

Sweetheart Summer

and-white cat attached itself to Lauren and followed her
everywhere. Lauren begged Sawyer to keep the cat, but he
insisted pets were too much work and responsibility. Lauren
had been heartbroken, but Sawyer wouldn't change his mind.
He wouldn't change his mind about Craft Mart, either.

Katie clenched and unclenched her fingers in her work
gloves and eyed the bench seat. "Can you help me with this
bench seat? I've been trying to get it out, and it won't budge.
Maybe if we both pull on it." It was easier to think about the
bench seat than to worry about what would happen to her
store with Craft Mart moving into town.

Ivy stepped to the right side as Katie slipped her hand
into the thin slot between the seat and the side wall. She
positioned herself so she could use her body weight as
leverage and grasped the edge of the bench. Ivy grabbed the
other end and both tugged. The seat still didn't move an inch.

"I've got to get a jimmy to get this loose." She needed to
keep working on the trailer, and the hardware store wouldn't
be open until Monday. Sunday was the only day she didn't
open the shop, and she planned to work on the trailer. She
didn't want to still be trying to find that last mouse on
Monday. Lights glowed from the home across the field and
the smell of barbecue drifted across.

"I'm going to see if Sawyer has a crowbar," Katie said to
Ivy.

Ivy raised an eyebrow. "Are you sure you're not going to
hit him with that crowbar?"

Katie laughed. "I'd like to, but I've got to finish this, and
the hardware store isn't open. I don't want to wait any
longer."

"Do you want me to go with you?" Ivy put up her fists.
"You might need a referee."

"I'll be fine." Katie hugged Ivy. "I'm a big girl, and I play
fair." She tossed her gloves on the counter. Her nerves rattled
and did nothing to calm the feelings shaking inside her.

Feelings that always lay dormant until confronted with conflict, and then they rushed back, reminding her of days spent hiding from her father. She was far from fine, but she couldn't hide from Sawyer, either. He was doing work on her barn. He was Lauren's father. And he was her neighbor. She might as well face him now.

"I'll see you in the morning. We'll get a group of people together and see what we can do at the council meeting to stop his fireworks show. He won't get away with everything without a fight." Ivy hugged Katie and headed for her car as Katie stepped into the field. The old garden gate that stood between her home and Sawyer's house remained closed with a rusted chain and lock. Even so, both Katie and Lauren found ways around the gate through a large hole in the fence on the far left side of the pasture.

The sun had dropped low enough in the sky to turn the fading sunlight yellow and gold. She ran her fingers through the tall grasses as they shimmered beneath her hands. She always strolled the fields when she had a problem she couldn't figure out. The wide open spaces cleared her mind and allowed new ideas and thoughts to emerge and fill her with a sense of hope and possibility. She tossed back her shoulders and steeled herself. She would have to make Sawyer see the importance of community and connection in Cranberry Bay. It was her only hope for saving her shop.

Chapter Six

Sawyer flipped a steak on the grill. He brushed a light layer of barbecue sauce over the meat before moving on to the next one. The setting sun cast long shadows across the patio. Birds chirped their final night song as the sky turned rose-colored.

Lisa sat at the round patio table and sipped a glass of pink lemonade from a mason jar. She shivered in the cool air and tightened a light green cardigan around her shoulders. Beside her, Maddie chattered about the design for the vintage market logo and promotional materials.

"You should sign up at the community college for a class in design," Lisa said. "They have great offerings in the summer for teens."

"I'd be happy to pay for it," Sawyer said. "It's always a good idea to get a start on some college classes. It looks good on the application."

"Katie!" Lisa exclaimed.

Katie? Sawyer frowned. What did Katie have to do with Maddie's design class? Startled, he looked up from the grill and into Katie's bright blue eyes. Before he could stop himself, he swept his glance over her paint-splattered T-shirt and tight shorts. His heart quickened, and his chest expanded.

"I'm sorry," Katie's cheeks flushed. "I didn't mean to interrupt a family dinner. I need to borrow a crowbar."

"A crowbar?" Sawyer raised an eyebrow.

"I can't get the bench seat out of the trailer." Katie wiped a strand of hair from her forehead. "Really, I didn't mean to interrupt. I can come back later." She turned to step off the patio.

"Wait. I'll see what I can find. The steaks are in a good spot and don't need my full attention right now." Sawyer said. But before he could head to his garage tool shop, Lauren's scream from the kitchen cut across the patio.

Sawyer dropped the basting brush in a small glass jar and hustled inside. "Lauren! What is it? Are you okay?" His heart pounded. Lately, it seemed like Lauren had been getting into a lot of accidents. So far nothing had resulted in a trip to the emergency room, but each time she screamed out in pain, his heart froze. If anything happened to his daughter, he didn't know how he would ever handle it. It'd been enough pain to lose Ginger; he could never imagine losing Lauren.

"I cut myself." Lauren stood in the middle of the kitchen with her finger in her mouth. Big tears ran down her cheeks. Torn lettuce lay strewn on the granite counter and on the floor beneath her. She took her finger out of her mouth and waved it in the air.

Sawyer picked up her hand. "I don't see anything." He frowned at her.

"It's right here." Lauren shoved her hand in his face. She wiggled her fingers.

"Let me see." Katie stepped up beside Sawyer. He inhaled sharply as she brushed against him emitting what seemed to be electric heat, hotter than the gas grill outside.

"Katie! " Lauren exclaimed. "I'm making the salad. Will you help me?"

Sawyer raised an eyebrow at Lauren. "I thought you hurt yourself."

"I'm all better now," Lauren said and smiled. "Cuts heal really fast."

"Mm …" Sawyer frowned. "I'm not so sure. I'd feel better if we could get a bandage on your finger and clean it up a bit."

"Katie can help me, right?"

"I can help you clean up the cut, but I really don't want to barge in on your family dinner. I just stopped by to borrow a tool."

"I really want you to stay," Lauren said, winding her arms around Katie's middle. "Please."

"We have more than enough food," Sawyer said, clearing his throat. "I'll pop another steak on the grill. Lauren needs someone to help her with the salad." He pushed away the nagging thought that he wanted her to stay just as much as Lauren did.

"I need to check the steaks," Sawyer said to Lauren. "Do you think you can take care of the salad with Katie?"

Lauren twirled to the tall kitchen pantry and opened it. She yanked a large black-and-white men's apron off a hook. "We don't have another apron. But, you can wear Dad's. He won't mind." She pushed the apron into Katie's hands.

Katie reached for the apron, but the fabric fluttered out of her hands to the floor, and Sawyer leaned down to pick it up. As he handed it to her, their fingers touched. A spark passed between them as Katie took the apron and slipped it on over her head. She reached around to tie it, and Sawyer stepped up behind her. "Let me." He took the ties from her and tied them around her small waist, inhaling her sweet scent and trying to stop himself from running his hands through her thick curly hair.

Lauren grinned and said, "It's a little big. But it'll do."

"I'll get another steak on the grill," Sawyer mumbled as he opened the refrigerator and pulled out another steak. The cool air felt good on his flushed face. Without looking at Katie, he closed the refrigerator door and picked up a plate that held zucchini, squash, and tomatoes on long skewers. He strode across the living room to the open patio doors.

"I'm sorry, but I think we're going to have to take a rain check on dinner." Lisa stood in the doorway leading off the patio to the living room. She unzipped her patchwork purse and pulled out a set of keys.

"There's a barn sale Mom promised to take me to. It's the last hour, and everything will be really cheap or free." Maddie added, "I'm working on a display with an old-fashioned Fourth of July theme for my booth at the vintage show."

"She scoured Mom's attic and came up with an old scrapbook of pictures of us riding in Dad's Studebaker," Lisa shook her head. "We had a good time in those parades." Her voice turned soft.

"We should get the truck out and ride in it this Fourth of July," Maddie said. "I bet everyone would love to see the old truck again, and we'd have so much fun." She clapped her hands together like a small child. Her eyes glowed.

The image of Dad's 1948 black Studebaker truck flashed across Sawyer's mind. His Dad loved vintage cars and trucks, and he never missed an opportunity to pull out his Studebaker and take it for a spin in the local parades and summer car shows up and down the coast. But Sawyer had never taken it out, unable to face the feelings of guilt he had over the final conversation they'd had minutes before Dad died of a heart attack. The day would always be etched in Sawyer's mind as the day when he'd taken his first drink and found himself filled with false bravado and belligerence.

"Don't you think that'd be a good idea?" Maddie pressed. "We could even wear period-style clothing."

"No." Sawyer said sharply and dropped the barbecue brush into the jar. It missed and toppled over the side and landed on the patio stone with a loud crash, leaving a small trace of red sauce on the sides of the grill.

"Sorry," Sawyer muttered, embarrassed by the strength of his emotions. It was one of the problems with not drinking. His anger seemed to bubble to the surface more than he liked. Sawyer caught a glimpse of Katie's pale face. She looked like she'd seen a ghost.

"Katie?" Sawyer asked.

"I'm fine." She turned and laid a place setting on the table. Her left hand shook slightly.

Sawyer frowned. Katie was not fine. "I didn't mean ..." Sawyer stopped as Katie took two placemats and sets of utensils off the table. She held them against her chest, as if keeping a barrier against Sawyer. Her eyes met his and a flash of vulnerability crossed her face. Gone was the tough female exterior he had seen so often at City Council meetings, and in its place was a fragility that made him want to reach out and drop his hand over her shoulder and pull her close to him. He mentally reminded himself to hold his anger in better check when around her.

"Here is the salad!" Lauren walked out the double French doors with a large wooden bowl filled with salad and a pair of tongs. She placed the bowl on the table. "You sit here," Lauren directed as she pointed to the chair next to her. "Dad will sit on the other side of you."

Sawyer set the plate of steaks on the table and pulled out the chair next to Katie. He was careful not to bump against her or the table as he stretched his long legs alongside hers. "I never quite have a home for these things," he said, tapping his legs and hoping to lighten the tension radiating from Katie's still form beside him.

She relaxed her shoulders and smiled. "I don't have that problem." She touched her legs, tucked neatly under the table.

Sawyer couldn't help but eye her tanned legs appreciatively. Even in her dirty denim shorts, she had a way of looking amazing. He reached over and picked up the plate of meat. His arm brushed against hers, but she didn't pull away. "Steak?"

Katie nodded, and Sawyer placed the thick juicy piece of meat on her plate. He set the second steak on Lauren's plate. She promptly picked up her steak knife and cut a large piece, which she stuck in her mouth and chewed. Sawyer licked his lips. He'd never been very good at making conversation and usually didn't have to worry about it. When Ginger had been alive, she'd always been the one to entertain their guests with lively stories and light chatter. After she died, a few drinks and his drinking-loosened tongue did just fine. He didn't usually remember what he'd said the next morning, but at least he always felt like he was a good conversationalist. But now he was as awkward as a teenage boy, unsure what to say to the pretty girl he had a crush on.

"The vintage market," Sawyer said, hoping the market would be something Katie could talk about easily. "You're selling items that belonged to someone else? Garage-sale-type things?"

Katie cut a small piece of meat. She held her fork above the plate. "I guess that's one way of looking at it."

"What's the other way?" Sawyer asked, and smiled at the tone he knew so well from their positions on opposite sides of the table. His stomach relaxed, and the tension unrolled from his shoulders.

"The other way," Katie said, sounding as if she was instructing one of her sewing students, "is these are repurposed items. Instead of going to fill a landfill, we are showing people how to reuse items they might have inherited or gotten from someone else."

Sawyer pointed his fork toward the rusted-closed garden gate that divided their two properties. "You mean the old gate would be something people would buy?"

"Yes." Katie nodded. "The gate could be one of our featured items. We'd place it in a display with other things people might use outside in gardens. With a few flowers and strategically placed with other items, the gate could do very well."

Sawyer shook his head. "But why not buy a new gate or new gardening tool?"

"People want to give an old-fashioned feel to their homes," Katie said, her voice slow and lilting as if recording a commercial. "It makes them feel connected to the past. Connected to generations before them."

Sawyer's stomach contracted as he stared toward his home. He worked hard not to feel connected to the past. And yet the past confronted him at every turn. The baby grand piano in the living room had belonged to Ginger, but no one played. The upstairs library was filled with her books, but he kept it closed all the time. And the third-floor craft room was never opened, and he made sure it was locked. And, his stomach clenched again, his dad's Studebaker was in his garage. His past lay around him in a display, frozen in time.

The sun set, and shadows darkened the patio. Katie grabbed a small pack of matches beside a large mason jar in the center of the table. She reached in and pulled out the white candle. Lighting it, she placed the candle back inside the jar, sending a small arc of light across the table. Lauren's sleeve draped close to the barbecue sauce on her plate, and Katie reached over and gently guided his daughter's arm away.

Sawyer pulled his thoughts away from the past as his heart skipped a beat. Why had he never noticed the glow Katie radiated? He had been so busy fighting her that he had failed to see the way she turned her head up, listening to everything that was said carefully before answering. Or the way her eyes shone in the dim light. Or the laughter that bubbled up from inside her as she listened to Lauren recount a humorous story. He'd only been able to see one side of her, the side that opposed him, but now, with her sitting beside him, there seemed to be so much more to her. So much more he wanted to get to know.

As if she felt the heat radiating from his heart, Katie glanced up. Their eyes met. He couldn't say a word as he felt himself pulled into the soft reflection of the candlelight in her eyes.

Katie broke the gaze and turned. She pointed to the setting sun across the field. "I used to love to walk in that field in the morning; I enjoyed seeing it in every season."

Sawyer heard the grief in Katie's voice and said quietly, "You can use the field anytime you want."

He remembered sitting at the table with his team of lawyers while Katie's aunt and uncle signed the paperwork to sell the farm. Forest Samson's hands only shook slightly. Sawyer hadn't stopped to think that this was their family farm they were selling. At the time, he'd been sky high about his life. He had a large bank account from his housing development in Seashore Cove, and he'd just married Ginger. He'd cut back on his drinking, and although loved a good party, he was able to control himself. It hadn't occurred to him that all of that could change. Or that he was just as vulnerable to life's ups and downs as the next person. Now he heard it all in Katie's voice. He reached out and touched the top of her hand.

"Daddy!" Lauren jumped up and tapped his sleeve. "You and Katie haven't finished your dinner, and we have brownies for dessert." She rubbed her stomach and licked her lips.

Sawyer chuckled and removed his hand from Katie's.

"You're right." Katie took a large bite of the salad. "This is the best salad I've ever tasted. I can't wait to eat those brownies."

Lauren twirled around the patio. "Katie can come for dinner any night, right Dad?"

Sawyer swallowed hard. "Yes," he said, his voice sounded gruff as their eyes locked and a glimmer of passion leapt between them in the shadows cast by candlelight.

Chapter Seven

The next evening, Katie opened the door to City Hall. The small chamber buzzed with conversation as Cranberry Bay citizens clustered together in small groups and filled Styrofoam cups with coffee. She picked up an agenda from the front table as Beth pushed a plate of raspberry pie into her hands. Beth wore a gingham apron with pie applique across the front bib. Two red-and-pink ribbons hung down the front with her rhinestone-framed glasses clipped to them.

"Try this." Beth handed her a plastic fork. "It's my great-grandmother's recipe, and it can't be beat."

"Oh yes it can." Sasha pushed her way past the table and gave Katie a thick slice of apple pie. "This is my great-grandfather's recipe, and it won the Oregon State Fair pie contest for three years."

Katie smiled at both women and balanced the plates on top of each other in her left hand. She made her way to a folding chair in the front of the room. She was careful to stay clear of Tyler, who dodged about the crowded room and handed out small slips of paper in the shape of pies with letters written across: "Vote for Sasha." One of Beth's twin granddaughters circulated on the other side of the room and handed out bookmarks with Beth's picture and name written across the center.

Katie sat down in the front seat and placed one of the plates on the floor beneath her chair. She dropped her shoulder bag to the ground and forked a small piece of raspberry pie and slipped it into her mouth as Ivy sank into the seat beside her.

"This is worse than elections." Ivy balanced a plate of apple pie and a cup of coffee in her hands. "I'm going to gain ten pounds by the time this contest is over. They've got us trying pies at every event and meeting all over Cranberry Bay.

"It is pretty competitive," Katie nodded as she chewed the flaky crust. "But this is pretty good."

"Don't let Sasha hear you say that!" Ivy said. "But," she lowered her voice. "I have to agree. Beth's family raspberry pie recipe is one of the best I've ever tasted." Ivy leaned closer to Katie. "How did it go last night?"

"Fine." Katie forked a large piece of pie and shoved it in her mouth. The barbecue from the night before still left a warm spot in her memory. She had been surprised at how easily the conversation flowed and the dinner passed. She had wanted to talk to Sawyer about Craft Mart but instead found herself struggling to find the right way to approach the subject without destroying the mood of the cozy family dinner.

Ivy studied Katie's face. "Did you talk about Craft Mart?"

"No." Katie shook her head. "It just didn't seem like the right time. I didn't want to upset Lauren and get in an argument with Sawyer during dinner."

"Dinner?" Ivy raised an eyebrow. "You stayed for dinner? I thought you were going to borrow a crowbar to fix the bench seat in the trailer?"

"Lauren needed help with her salad," Katie said. "She asked me to stay."

"Mm …" Ivy took a swallow of her coffee and grimaced. "I wish they'd learn how to make better coffee at these things."

Katie cleared her throat and looked at her notes, glad that Ivy had not continued to press her about last night. Sasha plopped into the chair next to Katie. She adjusted her raspberry-spotted apron across her lap. "Did you see what Sawyer is proposing now? Four days of a bright spotlight and an evening of fireworks for the opening of Liberty Bay Square."

"The fireworks won't pass the council." Katie said, and quickly steeled herself for the job at hand, grateful to be back on solid ground talking about Sawyer and how to oppose another one of his projects. She'd had a nice time at dinner, but Sawyer didn't change. She knew that more than anyone. She wasn't going to be lulled by his charms at one barbecue. She reached into her patchwork bag and pulled out a yellow tablet. She had filled the top half with codes that forbade fireworks and extensive lights and noises on any day of the year but the Fourth of July. She eyed the circular table at the front of the room. At least one of the councilwomen also served on the Parks Department board and could be counted on to want to protect nesting birds.

"I hope not," Ivy said. "No one wants a blazing spotlight across the quiet, moonlit fields for four nights or an extra night of fireworks set off simply to draw attention to large stores."

"I've got a few objections that I think will work for our cause." Katie tapped her paper as the mayor pounded his gavel and the room settled.

"Good evening, ladies and gentlemen. Thank you for coming out for the council meeting. I'm glad we can offer such fine entertainment at our meetings."

The room filled with chuckles, and Katie settled back in her chair. She loved council meetings. Nothing filled her with more pleasure then seeing the people of Cranberry Bay discuss an issue that would affect the town she loved and called home. One day, she hoped to fill her own seat at the front of the room and help implement decisions that would impact future residents of the small town.

"The first order of business is Sawyer Shuster with an application for fireworks for the Grand Opening of his Liberty Bay Square." Mays read from his agenda. "Sawyer?" Mays glanced toward the back of the room.

Sawyer strode to the podium, and the tempo in Katie's pulse increased. She took a long deep breath and placed her finished pie plate on the floor under her chair. Her stomach clenched with emotions she didn't want to think about, and she didn't reach for the second piece of pie.

"I'd like to offer the town a special fireworks night," Sawyer began in what sounded like a well-rehearsed speech. "As you know, Cranberry Bay often struggles to fund the yearly July Fourth show."

"We missed it last year," Tom called from the back of the room.

"That's right," Sawyer said. "And unless we can raise an additional fifteen-thousand dollars in two weeks, we're going to miss it again this year."

"I hate driving to the beach. It's always so crowded on the roads back to Cranberry Bay," Julie Mays, the mayor's wife, said. "I just know there's going to be a bad accident."

Sawyer turned and smiled at the crowd. He swept his gaze over each face as if he were reassuring each person in the room.

Sasha crossed her arms over her chest and let out a small sigh. Ivy crossed her legs and shifted in her chair. Katie straightened and planted her feet firmly against the floor. She would not be swayed by his attempt to gather supporters. She knew the truth behind the man in front of them. He would do whatever it took to get what he wanted at any cost. She was always surprised by how many people at the council meeting could be swayed by his charm. Thankfully, the council did what they were supposed to do and held to the codes and regulations.

"What I'd like to propose is that the fireworks show be sponsored by Liberty Bay Square."

"That'd be fine with me," Tom said. "I've had some medical expenses and can't afford to donate as much for the show as I usually can."

The crowd murmured as excited voices discussed the possibility of a fireworks show in Cranberry Bay that didn't rely on donations from the small-businesses and locals. Katie had to admit a part of her sighed in relief at not being asked to contribute to the annual fireworks show. Especially this year when everything was so tight with her finances. But at the same time, implementing a last-minute show that would maneuver around the codes was not something she wanted Sawyer to be able to do. It would be only one more in a long list of ways he worked around the rules, somehow believing they didn't apply to him.

"Good. I think we can all agree that Cranberry Bay would like to have a fireworks show this year that is not funded by the small businesses." Sawyer turned back to face the six members of the council. "I've got all the permits from the county, and I just need the city's approval. Once I have that, I'll go ahead and get the fire marshal to take a look and we should be good to go."

"Thank you, Sawyer," Mays said. "Your plan is appreciated. Any objections?"

Katie smoothed her hands over her slacks and stood. It was never easy to be the voice of dissent when the town wanted to support something. Although she had gotten used to it over the years, her stomach still churned when conflict arose in the meetings. Quietly, Katie reminded herself she was fighting for a larger cause. She was fighting to stop Sawyer from slowly creeping in and ruining the town with his big businesses and money, with little regard for the people. If she had any doubt he harbored any other plans, all she had to do was look at his recent decision to slip Craft Mart into his store line-up.

Katie slipped around Ivy and out the row of chairs to the podium. Her arm brushed against Sawyer as she took her place, and he stepped out of the way. A small shiver sliced through her middle, and she quickly busied herself with adjusting the mic and forcing herself to focus.

Katie leaned forward and spoke clearly. "I'd like the council to seriously consider denying this application. Code CB2354 states that fireworks must be permitted a year in advance. As it is only weeks until the July Fourth holiday, this is not possible with this application."

"I object to the allegation of a code violation." Sawyer stepped to the podium, and Katie moved aside, struggling not to touch him. "In the case of the town's fireworks, yes, the application must be permitted a year in advance. However," he glanced down at a thick sheet of papers, "this is for a shopping mall opening. It fits into the category of permits allowed for special occasions."

Katie stiffened. Why did Sawyer always find a loophole in everything?

"I believe Sawyer is correct," Councilman Jeff Peterson said. "The fireworks fall under the special occasion permits. Same thing for the spotlight."

"Are there any more objections?" the mayor asked.

"No." Katie slipped back to her seat. She clenched her jaw and dropped her folder into her bag. She tried to remind herself that not all fights with Sawyer resulted in wins. Sometimes he did have the correct codes lined up. But this one seemed unbearably hard. It was enough he had been able to slip Craft Mart into his development at the last minute, but now he was enticing the town's patriotic side by offering the only fireworks option for Cranberry Bay on the July Fourth holiday.

Ivy reached under Katie's seat and pulled out the uneaten apple pie. "Always good for cheering you up," she whispered.

Katie forked the piece of pie with more force than necessary. She could have eaten the whole pie. She stared straight ahead of her and shoved a large piece of apple pie into her mouth.

"The second order of business tonight is Josh with the historic railroad association and Adam with the parks department," Mays said.

Josh moved from the side of the room. When he reached the podium, he stopped and clicked on a large button placed on the wall behind him. A large picture filled the front screen behind the council members and showed colorful makeshift bike trails with cartoon characters riding bikes. Beside Katie, Ivy giggled and clamped her hand over her mouth like a schoolgirl with a crush.

Josh grinned at her, and his ears turned red. "It's not a great representation, but what I hope it shows is how we plan to use the old railroad tracks as bike trails."

"Where will the funding come from?" Mays asked.

"Adam?" Josh took a step backward as Adam stepped beside Josh and took the microphone.

Adam cleared his throat and ran his hand through his thick curly hair. His cheeks turned such a bright red, Katie couldn't help but smile. The youngest Shuster brother had been in her class in school, and he'd always been nervous giving speeches. He'd quickly taken to the parks and trails in the surrounding mountains, and it surprised no one to see him take on the job of the parks department's head ranger. "The parks department has recently obtained a grant from the county. We'd like to use this grant for this project."

"That looks like a great idea," Mays studied the picture. "How far out will the trails go? And will there be anything at the end of the trails?"

"Sawyer?" Josh turned and motioned for Sawyer to step forward.

Sawyer. Katie chewed hard. Why was Sawyer involved in this project? Parks and trails and bikes didn't seem like something that would bring Sawyer into the picture. There was no money to be made, only spent.

Sawyer took his place alongside Josh. He cleared his throat and shuffled his feet. His cheeks sported two red spots, and Katie studied him. Was he nervous? She'd never seen Sawyer nervous at a council meeting. Katie leaned forward in her chair. What was making Sawyer so nervous speaking to a room he had commanded only minutes ago?

Sawyer cleared his throat again. "I'd like to donate a portion of my property to the parks department for use at the end of the trails. It'd make a nice nature preserve, and people could enjoy picnics while watching the birds."

Katie froze as her throat contracted in a quick rush of unshed tears. Sawyer wanted to donate a part of the land that had once belonged to her family to the parks department? She would not see a field full of houses beside her. She would see the grassy fields and rich farmlands filled with families at picnics. What could have gotten into Sawyer to make this decision? Fireworks were one thing but donating a portion of his land?

"That's very generous of you," Mays said as the six council members nodded their heads and the room exploded into claps and murmurs.

Adam clicked the button on the wall, and a new slide appeared on the screen. "We'd like to connect the trails on the railroad tracks out to Sawyer's land. It has quite a bit of wetlands on it, so it will need to be preserved with wooden bridges and trails over the land. We'll start work on it as soon as the permits are approved by the county, and, hopefully by next summer, we'll have everything in place."

Ivy leaned over to Katie. "This is too good to be true. What do you think Sawyer is up to?"

Katie shook her head. She didn't know what could be motivating Sawyer to give up his land as a donation. Sometimes developers did sell off wetlands to the county in exchange for other land they wanted to purchase to mitigate the impact. But, as far as she knew, the land they owned didn't have enough wetlands to make a difference. The bikes had made a splash in Cranberry Bay, and Lauren didn't have access to many of the trails living so far out of town. If the trails extended down to their property, Lauren could ride her bike not only on the trails but also to school and into the small town to see her friends. Puzzled, Katie gazed at Sawyer as he stepped away from the podium. He glanced over at her and smiled shyly, and her heart crashed to her painted toes.

Chapter Eight

"I'll send the papers for the land over this afternoon," Sawyer spoke on the phone to lawyer and family friend, Jack Perkins He turned off his Bluetooth headset and headed toward the trailer on the side of the barn. He felt good about donating seven acres of his property to the parks department. It would help mitigate the fees he'd pay as a developer when it came time to build the cottage-home development, something he hoped to get started on as soon as Liberty Bay Square cleared a bit of profit over the next few months. Plus the trails stretching to the outskirts of town would help Lauren ride her bike into town and to school on nice days. But there was something else eased in him. He had gotten the land at a fire sale price. Katie's aunt and uncle had wanted only to get out of Cranberry Bay and retire to Florida. The land had been for sale for over two years, and both were tired of holding on. They'd agreed to pretty much everything he wanted, including a lowball price. But the guilt had eaten away at Sawyer. Now, some of that guilt eased.

Sawyer went up the small trailer's steps and ducked his head at the doorway. "Katie?"

A metal box of tools sat on bright-yellow cushions for the bench seats. Yellow-and-white curtains hung on the open windows over the table. A matching yellow flag-shaped banner hung from the curtain rod and blew lightly in the breeze. Outside the window, a hummingbird fed on a vine of yellow honeysuckle along a wooden fence. The sweet scent carried on the wind and drifted through the windows. Small birds darted in and out of the green suet feeder hanging on a nail. Their chirping song floated into the camper.

"Yes?" Katie stood in the middle of the black-and-white checkered floor, hands on her hips. She surveyed a round table.

"I was thinking the barn needed a new coat of paint. I've got some discounts lined up at the paint store. I'd be happy to pick up some gallons of red and get it on the boards for you." The weatherworn boards screamed for a new coat of paint. Nothing would look better than coming around the bend and seeing the bright red barn.

Katie frowned at him. "I don't want to paint the barn red."

"It'd be better for business," Sawyer said, leaning back on his heels and studying Katie. "A red barn will catch people's eyes if they're coming out here for the vintage markets."

"No," Katie said firmly in the voice Sawyer knew so well. "The weathered look is part of the vintage appeal."

"I guess," Sawyer said. "But some of those boards need to be replaced. They're rotting."

"Fine." Katie nodded to him. "Replace the boards. But don't paint anything red."

Sawyer grinned and shook his head. Katie's determination didn't stop at the council meetings. He admired her passion and drive for her life and business. Although he enjoyed developing land, he didn't share the same passion. It was a way to make money, and he enjoyed making money, but it wasn't his heart and soul. Something inside him swelled and drew him toward her. "Need some help with the table?"

Katie nodded. "I don't want to scratch the floor, and I'm afraid if I try and move the table myself, I'll leave long scratches." Small beads of sweat pooled on her forehead. A line of sweat trailed down her red T-shirt. She grabbed a yellow scrunchie from her pocket. In one sweep, she pulled her hair into a messy bun on top of her head. Pieces stuck out at odd angles. Sawyer had never seen her look more beautiful. He swallowed hard and stumbled on the last step into the trailer.

"Careful." Katie grabbed his right forearm as he steadied himself.

"I'm okay." Sawyer's voice sounded gruff. "I think I just missed a step." He stared at Katie's hand still resting on his arm. It seemed unseasonably warm in the camper, although a breeze blew through all the open windows.

Sawyer grasped the edges of the table. "Ready?"

Katie stepped around the table and lifted the opposite end. She took two steps backward and placed the table between the two bench seats. There was just enough space for Katie to shimmy around the sides. She eyed the space. "That looks like it fits." She grabbed a circular cloth from a bench seat and shook it out. Sawyer took one end, and, together, they placed it over the table.

"Where'd you find the vintage yellow appliances?" Sawyer ran his hand over the front of the refrigerator. "I haven't seen things like this since I was a kid."

"Ivy found them," Katie said. "A family in the valley called her. They kept a trailer in the back of their house for years. Ivy and I drove down to take a look. The trailer had serious water damage and couldn't be salvaged, but I was able to grab the refrigerator, stove, and some cabinets."

"The table works perfectly here." He gazed past the table at the large double bed in the back of the camper. A rag quilt in yellow-and-pink matched the curtains hanging along the back window above the bed. Large, thick pillows placed along the back wall made him want to lay down and take a long nap. He imagined himself curled up with Katie. Her soft body pressed against his as he held her in his arms. The moonlight streaming in through the open windows.

"It just won't fit." Katie shoved her left side against the small stove. "I couldn't get it to turn on, so I pulled it out. But now I can't get the table to fit back, and it still won't turn on. I don't know what's wrong."

"Let me take a look." Sawyer didn't have a lot of room to maneuver in the small kitchen area. As he stepped beside Katie, her body brushed against his. Maybe he'd been wrong to insist on such a large kitchen in his home.

Katie placed her hands on the stovetop. "The stove came from the same year trailer as this one. We tried it out before we loaded it into Ivy's truck, and everything worked fine."

"It's an electric stove, so you shouldn't need to fill your propane tank." Sawyer reached his hand into the back and fiddled with the cords. "The cord is a little loose."

Katie sank down on the bench seat. She wiped her hand over her forehead. Dark circles lined her eyes. "Can it be fixed?"

"Let me check." Sawyer crouched down and rolled over on his side. "This thing isn't plugged in, is it?" The last thing he needed was an electric shock.

"It's not plugged in. The cord is by you," Katie said, as a smile coated her voice. "You don't trust me?"

"No," Sawyer said, and smiled as he fiddled with the wire. "Do you have a pair of pliers?"

"Here you go." Katie handed it to him. Her eyes sparkled as she leaned over the stove and dangled the pliers above his head. He propped himself up and grabbed for the pliers. She waved it in the air for a minute before lowering them to him. Their fingers touched, and Sawyer swore he felt the electric shock of something that was very plugged in.

Sawyer attached the pliers to the wire, and gave it a few turns. He hummed as he worked. It felt good to help out. Katie juggled a lot. The store and the vintage market, and she always had her hands in the town's various causes and events. She'd helped him with Lauren for the last few years, and he'd never acknowledged it. It was time to start being a better neighbor and helping her out more. Something inside him tugged. Something that turned over in his heart. He wasn't falling in love with her. That would be silly. He was just helping out a neighbor.

After the wire was fitted neatly into the slot, Sawyer reached along the side for the cord. His fingers found it, and he plugged it in. Sawyer rolled over and sat up. "That should do it."

Katie stepped beside the stove and reached out her hand to him.

Sawyer entwined his fingers with hers and pulled himself to standing, careful not to give her his weight. He stared into her eyes. Why had he never realized how much they sparkled and drew him into their depths? Or, as his gaze dropped along her face, how much he wanted to kiss her soft lips and feel her body against his?

Gently, Katie released her hand and left emptiness where her fingers had once been entwined with his.

Sawyer forced himself to push away his conflicting feelings. He could not be falling for Katie. He only wanted to help her get a few things done for the market. But something inside him twisted. There was a lot about Katie that he wanted to get to know.

Quickly, he grabbed both sides of the stove and maneuvered it into place. As he withdrew his hands, his wrist caught on a small metal hook on the side. The sharp pain caused him to flinch as a trickle of blood ran down his wrist.

"You're hurt!" Katie pressed beside him as she grabbed a milk jug filled with water sitting beside the sink. "The water isn't working yet, but I've filled this jug with clean water from the house. Stand over the sink."

"I'll just run to the hose outside." Sawyer held his hand by his side. "Don't worry about it."

"No." Katie's voice arched upward in a direct command. "You've hurt yourself in my trailer. I'll take care of you." Katie unscrewed the top of the milk jug and poured a slow trickle over his cut.

Sawyer leaned against the counter, his thighs pressed into the cabinet handles. He tried to steady himself. It wasn't the cut making him woozy. It was the nearness of Katie and her touching him, kind, gentle, and yet firm. He couldn't remember the last time he had felt such a gentle touch. Sawyer sank down on the bench, being careful not to get the new yellow fabric dirty. He'd never been a fan of blood. Every Halloween, Adam and Bryan loved to dress up using gauze and bandages from Dad's medical supply cabinet in his office. They had a great time creating red food coloring and ketchup mixtures to paste all over themselves before chasing each other out into the dark fall night to go trick-or-treating. Sawyer had never participated in his brothers' gory fun. He chose instead to be a knight or a king with items found in the dress-up box Mom kept in the attic for Lisa and her friends.

Katie emerged from the bathroom with a light green washcloth. She took his wrist and carefully dried the wound.

Sawyer wanted to moan in pleasure as she wrapped the cloth around his wrist and applied a light pressure, but he bit the impulse back. "I get on the roof and don't hurt myself, but one tiny push of that stove, and I've got a bloody mess," Sawyer joked, trying to make light of the situation and distract himself from Katie's touch.

Katie smiled and said, "I'm surprised I haven't managed to hurt anything myself. It was a real challenge getting that bench out of there." She gazed at him. Her eyes were soft. "Thanks to your crowbar, I was able to pull it out easily."

"Keep it until you're done. You might need it again," Sawyer said.

"I hope I'm all done with the hard part of the trailer rehab. But thank you." Katie unwrapped the cloth and squeezed a small amount of antibiotic ointment from a tube. "This might sting. But Mom always swore it was the best thing for cuts."

Sawyer placed his good hand on the edge of the seat and braced himself for the sting. It didn't happen. Instead, Katie's gentle and cool fingers massaged the ointment into Sawyer's wrist. His body relaxed as she smoothed the lotion back and forth.

"Band-Aid?" Katie held up a box of bandages.

"Sure," Sawyer said. "As long as it's not dinosaurs or fishes." He pictured the box of bandages his mom kept in the bathroom closet. He suspected one of the reasons Lauren liked to get hurt so often was because she enjoyed seeing what type of animal her grandmother had handy.

Katie giggled. "No. Regular old Band-Aid." She unwrapped a package and placed the sticky strip on his cut. "I think you're good to go."

But Katie didn't move, and his gaze drifted from her eyes, down her cheeks, to her lush lips.

Unable to stop himself any longer, Sawyer lowered his head toward those lips. "Katie," he whispered. His lips brushed against hers.

"Anyone here?" Ivy clattered up the trailer steps. Bags jostled by her sides. Her cheeks flushed with excitement. "You're never going to believe what I found!"

Startled, Katie pulled away from him. Sawyer blinked his eyes and tried to refocus. He had been about to kiss Katie. How had that happened? Sunlight streamed through the windows and bounced off the bench seats onto the floor in long arcs of light as he tried to clear his mind.

"I found matching kitchen canisters. They'll be perfect." Ivy stared at Sawyer and then Katie. "Am I interrupting?"

"No," Sawyer said at the same time as Katie. Their voices joined together in one high arc and filled the small space.

"Mm …" Ivy plopped a large basket on the table filled with all shapes and sizes of colorful canisters and clear mason jars. "I grabbed all the canisters and jars I could find at the garage sale. Everyone thought I was a little crazy." She shook her head, and her long hair trailed across her back.

"Great." Katie stepped away from Sawyer and peered into the basket. She lifted out two glass jars and filled each with water from the jug. When the jars were filled, she grabbed a packet of food coloring from a small drawer beside the stove. She dropped a few drops of blue in one and red in the other. Afterward, she took a few daisies from a large bucket and filled the jars with them, the water giving a pretty red, white, and blue look.

Sawyer stood and placed his hands in his pockets. He needed to leave and let the women work on the market items, but something inside him didn't want to go.

"I got our market application filed with the city." Katie picked up a flowered dishtowel. She hung it on a silver rack under the sink. "Everything looks good."

"What about the parking?" Ivy pulled canisters from the basket and eyed them, searching for cracks that might make them unsellable.

"We'll have to use the church parking lot. The high school is filled with the tournament. No one can do anything up there that weekend. It'll take away from our profit to have a shuttle, but there isn't much else we can do." Katie turned and crossed her hands over her chest. She leaned against the sink.

"You can use my field," Sawyer said. "We'll get a couple of the boys from the high school baseball team to collect money for you from each car. This way, you're taking in money and not shelling it out."

"You're going to let us park in your field?" Ivy stared at Sawyer as if he were an alien. She waved her hand out the window. "The whole field?"

"Sure," Sawyer said. "It's not a problem. We're going to be reconstructing the property with the land donation to the parks soon. It'll be fine to start tearing up the grass with car parking now."

Ivy peered at him. "I don't know what's gotten into you lately. First the donation and now the use of your field." She shook her head.

"I'm just trying to be part of the community," Sawyer said quietly. And he realized, with a start, there was something about Katie that brought out a feeling in him of wanting to be a part of things. He wanted to be connected to the small town. He wanted to be as he had been as a boy and teenager, someone the community loved and respected. And he was going to start doing what it took to make that happen.

Chapter Nine

Katie closed the fabric shop door and dropped the key in her patchwork purse. A small headache pulsed between her eyes. She'd spent the last hour working on the books. The summer classes had done well with enrollment. But no matter how she scrunched and crunched the numbers, she still didn't have enough to cover the upcoming fabric orders she needed to place for the fall season. And things were not going to get better. Craft Mart would open in a few weeks, and her customers would drift to the discounts and coupons.

Ivy rode up beside Katie on her light blue one-speed bike. "Are you coming to the concert tonight? It's the Wild Rose country band that is so popular at Seashore Cove."

"Yes," Katie said. "I wouldn't miss it." Across the street, people gathered for the first summer concert in the park. Families carried picnic baskets, coolers, and lawn chairs. Children and teenagers rode bikes up and down the newly installed bike paths running along the perimeter of the park. Jason Steidel directed cars as they drove slowly down Main Street and turned into the parking lot beside the old railway station.

Josh whistled and motioned to Ivy. "Ivy!" he hollered over the street noise. "Are you coming to help?"

Ivy placed both feet on the ground and steadied her bike between her skirted legs. The tulips in her basket tilted and wobbled. "I promised Josh I'd help him hand out some of the train brochures. He's got to fix a track before we get to the fall season." She fiddled with her handlebars. "He didn't want to hold a fundraiser and take away from the school's auction, so he's hoping to entice people to buy new memberships by naming a seat after them in the train car."

"Great idea." Katie straightened the flowers in Ivy's basket. "These are fake?" Katie plucked one of the tulips from the basket and dangled it in her fingers.

Ivy's eyes widened in surprise. She grabbed the greenery from Katie. "Of course. Did you think I'd spend money for fresh ones when I've got a ton of these things all over the store? All those discounts at the craft superstores. These things are at every garage sale." Ivy's eyes widened. "I'm sorry Katie. I didn't mean to …"

"It's okay," Katie said, waving away her friend's concern. "We've got to get used to it. Sawyer is bringing Craft Mart to Liberty Bay Square." Sawyer. She wanted to hate him. She desperately wanted to hate him. He was the man bringing in the store that would destroy her business.

But at the same time, he had donated some of his land for the parks, and he had been very supportive of the market. Was it possible he was having a change of heart about the small town? Did he harbor sentimental feelings for the place he had grown up after all? And what about her own growing feelings for him? She tried to deny them, but she couldn't help but find herself wondering what it would be like to kiss him and to be held in his arms. They'd come so close in the trailer, and she'd felt herself ache with a longing of unfilled desire when he pulled away.

Jason blew his whistle and held up his hand to stop the traffic. "That's jaywalking, Ivy. Next time use the crosswalk."

"Jay-biking!" Ivy waved.

Katie smiled at the lighthearted spirit dancing in air. It was always so good once summer got going in Cranberry Bay. Winters could be hard, with long, dark, rainy days, and spring seemed to take forever to arrive, the wind blowing cold with clear sunny days. By the time June arrived and the warmth poured in, everyone's spirits lifted and sprang to new life.

Ivy pedaled off to the park, and Katie strolled to Sasha's bakery, two doors down from the fabric shop. The geraniums and the petunias in the hanging baskets bloomed red, white, and blue. Each shop owner had filled the wooden planters lining the walls of the shops on Main Street with a host of flowers ranging from hydrangeas to large white daisies. A sidewalk chalkboard on an easel sat in front of Gracie's inn, announcing a summer midweek special. The aroma of freshly baked cranberry bread drifted from Sasha's bakery. Katie's heart contracted. What would she do when she had to give up her shop on Main Street and leave the spirit of friendship, community, and support that she had come to depend on?

As she reached the door, Sawyer crashed against her coming out of the bakery. He was furiously texting on his phone and didn't look up.

"Sawyer." Katie's heart pounded as their bodies touched, and she pressed her hands against his chest.

Katie." Sawyer looked down at her, his eyes softening as he slipped his phone into his pocket. "I'm sorry. I forgot to order Lauren a cake for her birthday. Sasha is swamped with orders and that pie contest. She's got six different pies on the counter but not one cake."

"She'll bake the cake." Katie nodded. No matter what, Sasha would come through with a birthday cake. She'd never let Lauren down. Even if it meant she'd have to stay up all night, she'd get the cake baked. That was what made Sasha so popular with all the locals. She worked hard to make sure everyone's special events were taken care of, even if it meant sacrificing her own holidays.

Rebecca Shuster and Jack rode by slowly on their bikes, heading for the park. Rebecca wore light-blue pedal pushers and a white cardigan over her pale peach blouse. She dinged a small bell on the front of her bike. "Coming through," she called out cheerily.

"Excuse us." Jack's deep voice boomed.

Sawyer waved to his mom and the family lawyer as he took a step back against the warm building. "It looks like everyone is on bikes," Sawyer said. He smiled down at her. His eyes warm. "Where's yours?"

Katie's heart turned over at the look in Sawyer's eyes. He did not remove his arm from her side, and she made no effort to shift away from him. "It's in the back of the shop. I rode it to work this morning."

"You rode your bike all the way out from our place?" Sawyer's voice took on a note of astonishment. His eyes caressed her and sent shivers to her stomach.

"Yes." Katie flushed. She knew he didn't mean our place, but something in that sounded nice. "It's an easy, flat road. There weren't a lot of cars until I got into town, and then I biked along the sidewalks coming down from the houses on the hill."

"You can't ride your bike home," Sawyer said firmly. "It'll be dark after the concert. I'll give you a ride. We can toss the bike in the back of my truck." He paused. "Want to take a walk? The music hasn't started yet. I bet the lower trail by the river won't be filled with too many people," he smiled at her, "or bikes."

"Sure." Katie hoped her voice sounded steady. It was only a walk. She took walks along the trail in the park all the time with Ivy, Sasha, and Gracie. They often used the park trails to clear their minds after long days in their businesses and to discuss new ideas. Her walk with Sawyer would be no different than her time with her girlfriends. Katie's heart contracted. If only butterflies didn't flutter in her stomach when she stepped up beside Sawyer.

At the end of Main Street, Bryan and Rylee made their way from the parking lot to the park with blankets and picnic basket in hand, their fingers linked. Bryan's real estate business and Rylee's staging and design were primary sponsors of the concert series. It'd been Rylee who had been able to influence the popular band, Wild Rose to play tonight. She'd brought a lot of her big city skills to Cranberry Bay, and they were paying off for everyone.

Katie and Sawyer waited at the crosswalk until the light turned to "Walk." They stepped off the curb and walked across the street to the lower edges of the park away, from the crowds gathering on the lawn by the stage. Sawyer placed his hand on Katie's lower back and steered her toward the marina dock. A wooden gazebo glowed, with small lights strung around the octagon at its top. A young teenage couple embraced at the far corner of the gazebo.

Katie had always loved the dock and gazebo in the summer. The gazebo often served as a backdrop for high school prom and senior pictures as well as the occasional Cranberry Bay wedding. The gazebo also functioned as the town's center for everything from first kisses to proposals. Her heart fluttered in her chest. If Sawyer was steering her toward the gazebo, did that mean he wanted to finish the kiss they'd almost shared in the camper? She knew she should resist him. She shouldn't allow him to get close enough to her to kiss her again. But a part of her was pulled so strongly to him, it was like being caught in a river's current.

As they reached the gazebo, Sawyer held out his hand to her. She slipped her fingers into his and took a step up the small stairway leading inside. The teenage couple quickly finished their kiss and, holding hands, strolled toward a bench in a darker corner of the park. The sound of the band warming up traveled down the hillside. Everything felt so safe and protected in Cranberry Bay.

"You love it here, don't you?" Sawyer asked as he guided her to the far end where they could look over the rushing river below. He gently caressed the top of her hand with his thumb, and Katie shivered at the touch.

"Yes." Katie stared into the river and leaned against the railing. Sawyer stood beside her. His body pressing against hers lightly. "I've always loved it here. I know what it's like in other places."

"What other places?" Sawyer's voice softened. He moved, so he stood closer to her, shielding her, protecting her.

"Mom and I were on the road for a year. We lived in the trailer. At first it was fun." Katie stopped, remembering how when they'd first set out, it was an adventure. "But then, when the fall storms came, it was just cold and scary. Mom finally called her sister, and she let us come live with them."

"At the dairy farm?"

Katie nodded. "The night we showed up, it was dark and raining. My aunt and uncle didn't want us here. The house was too small, but they took us in. They knew we didn't have anywhere else to go. They knew we had to escape from Dad."

Sawyer took a step behind Katie. He wrapped his arms around her and pulled her close. She leaned back against him and relaxed. "I'm sorry, Katie," Sawyer said. "I'm sorry you had to go through that."

Katie swallowed hard. The tears threatened to overtake her. She remembered the night she and Mom left Dad. He lay on the floor, passed out. They had stepped over him, each with one suitcase, and she had known she'd never see him again.

Katie shifted in Sawyer's arms and turned the conversation away from the pain that threatened to overtake her in one swallow. "You grew up here. Did you ever want to live anywhere else?"

Sawyer's voice deepened with emotion. "There was a time after Ginger died when I thought about just getting in the car and going somewhere, anywhere the memories wouldn't confront me at every turn. Her family moved about a year after she died, and I envied them. Their ability to just pick up and go to Portland and start over."

"But …"

"But I couldn't do it."

The words hung unspoken between them. Sawyer loved Cranberry Bay. In his own way, he loved the same small town she did. Katie's heart softened. His decision to bring development into Cranberry Bay wasn't because he was trying to destroy it. He was trying to save it in the only way he knew how.

The music burst into full song to a smattering of applause. "Want to dance?" Sawyer whispered against the top of her hair.

Turning, Katie stepped so she faced Sawyer, and his arms came around her. She inhaled deeply and felt the solidness of Sawyer's body against her.

Slowly, he moved to the music, and she stepped with him. They danced across the floor of the gazebo, her heart pounding in time with his.

The song ended, and she pulled away to look up at him. He lifted his finger and traced a line from her forehead to her lips. "Katie," he asked. "Can I kiss you?"

Katie could barely breathe. Her pulse raced, and she nodded as Sawyer lowered his lips to hers. She opened to him, the softness of his lips pressing against hers as she shifted against him and surrendered to his kiss.

Chapter Ten

Sawyer ran his hands through Katie's thick hair and deepened the kiss. She moaned softly beneath him, and he pressed closer to her.

"Sawyer!" Adam ducked into the gazebo. "Sorry to interrupt you." Adam cleared his throat. "We've been looking for you. The band's sound isn't working."

Sawyer pulled hesitantly away from Katie. He hadn't noticed the music had stopped. It seemed as if the music inside him increased as he kissed Katie's soft lips.

Beside him, Katie stepped back and smoothed her hands over her shorts.

"I've got to go." Sawyer nodded to Adam, who ducked out of the gazebo.

"Yes." Katie smiled at him, but her smile didn't reach to her eyes before she looked down at the ground, and he saw the flash of hurt cross her face.

"Katie ..." Sawyer broke off. He wanted to tell her the kiss wasn't a mistake. He wasn't pushing her away. The band broke into song but was quickly silenced with a loud screech to loud groans and boos. If the sound didn't get fixed soon, people might start tossing their picnics. Abruptly, Sawyer hustled out of the gazebo, where he caught up to Adam.

"Sorry." Adam peered at Sawyer. "I didn't want to interrupt you." He grinned. "But you're the only one who knows how the soundstage works. The band has been struggling for the last two songs. They took a quick intermission, so it could be fixed."

"No problem." Sawyer lengthened his stride. His emotions churned. Kissing Katie tonight had relit something in him, and his stomach quivered. He felt alive in a way he hadn't felt in years. But something else tugged at him. Katie deserved someone much better than a man like him. He pushed down the guilt harboring in his chest. But the memories flooded his mind. Too many nights spent drinking in the lower rooms of his home because he wasn't capable of being there for Ginger. Nights when he could have been with Ginger offering her comfort, but he, instead, drank himself into oblivion because he couldn't handle the pain of watching the woman he loved slip away from him, unable to do anything about it. How could he trust himself to be there for Katie? She deserved better, and he couldn't let himself get any closer.

Sawyer threaded through the crowd of people clustered on blankets and low-back lawn chairs on the grassy field. At the back of the stage, the band had moved offstage and was fiddling with guitars, cords, and amplifiers. "Sorry about the problems." Sawyer hustled up the small steps to the outlets. Long cords stretched from the stage to the plugs; various extension cords were plugged into the various pieces of equipment.

"Can it be fixed?" Adam leaned over his shoulder.

"I think there's too much plugged into this outlet." Sawyer yanked out a cord. "It's overloaded and is shorting out."

The lead singer, a tall thin man in his twenties, signaled to a guitar player for a sound check. The short dark-haired man strummed a few chords, and the crowd on the lawn cheered.

"We're good." Adam gave Sawyer a thumbs-up.

Sawyer nodded and double-checked the second outlet. After noting everything was working correctly, and the band was playing again, he hustled down the stairs. His foot caught a loose board, and he stumbled down the last stair. Sawyer leaned down and adjusted the board. He grabbed a roll of masking tape from the corner of the backstage wall and marked a large X across the stair to warn people about the loose board. He'd stop by tomorrow and nail it into place.

Sawyer strode along the edges of the front lawn. Night had settled into the park, and the stage lights glowed. The smell of sweet honeysuckle drifted from the vines along the park's fence. People sang along to the band's festive summer tunes, and children danced in the space below the stage.

A small hand touched his pants leg. "Dad!" Lauren said.

Sawyer stopped and smiled at his daughter, who was sprawled on a red-and-white checkered blanket. Brownie crumbs lay around her, and an open picnic basket had been tossed to the side. His mom sat in a lawn chair. A large straw hat on her head, a blue cardigan, and a full-length maxi-skirt draped around her legs. She had tossed a red blanket over her legs and tucked them beneath her in the low-back chair.

Sawyer knelt beside his mom. He spoke in a low voice. "Do you still want to take Lauren for the night?" Lauren loved the summer overnights at her grandma's house. Both loved the extended time spent together. But Rebecca had agreed to host Lauren's family birthday party the next afternoon, and he didn't want her to become too tired with Lauren's high energy.

"Of course!" His mom smiled at her granddaughter. "I wouldn't miss the special overnights for the world."

Sawyer squeezed his mom's shoulder. He leaned down to give her a slight kiss. "Thanks, Mom."

Sawyer turned and tapped Lauren on the arm. "I'll see you tomorrow after sewing camp, okay?"

Lauren reached over and embraced Sawyer in a large bear-hug.

Sawyer's heart cascaded into a pool of molten chocolate lava cake, and he hugged his daughter hard. "I love you," he said into her hair. There was no one who mattered more to him than his daughter.

"I love you too, Dad," Lauren said.

Sawyer unwound himself from Lauren's embrace as the song ended. He slipped through the crowd of people, now on their feet cheering for the next song, and headed out the park's east entrance onto First Street. For a minute, he couldn't help but look at the lighted pub, the firelight glowing on the back patio overlooking the river. He'd spent quite a few summer concerts sitting on the patio and listening to the band. It'd been a little different atmosphere than the crowd in the park, louder and more boisterous as the night went on.

The overnights with Lauren at his mom's house had begun because of a bad night at the pub. After he'd come out of a summer concert pub night, his mom had taken one look at him, wrapped her arm around Lauren, and suggested she spend the night with her. He'd stumbled back to the bar where Tricia had called for a safe ride for him. He barely remembered making it into bed that night and had been startled to find Lauren not with him the next morning. It'd taken a couple of quick phone calls to Bryan and his mom to figure out what had happened. His mom had never mentioned it to him, but afterward had simply started allowing Lauren to stay with her on summer concert series nights. It seemed the best way to protect Lauren from his drinking.

Sawyer shook his head. He wasn't going down that road again. Ever. Abruptly, he turned and headed toward home.

***

The next morning, Sawyer hustled down Main Street toward the New Leaf Sewing Shop. He hoped Lauren would be as excited about her birthday party as the family seemed to be. His phone had been lit all morning with preparation texts and e-mails. Nothing excited the Shuster clan more than a family get-together. As he passed the community church, Coach Simmons and several other men were gathered in small groups. They wore the same colored T-shirt with the slogan across the top, "One Day at A Time." Two small, white softball imprints outlined either end of the lettering. Coach had never made his longtime sobriety a secret. During Sawyer's days of playing high school baseball, Coach always made it clear he attended meetings as a sober alcoholic, and he never scheduled practices or game nights on meeting nights.

"Sawyer," Coach said. "We're looking for another person to join our team. Are you interested? It's a sober team."

"I don't think I'm up to it right now," Sawyer said. "Got a lot on my plate." The last thing he wanted was to go back to AA meetings or play on a sober team. He'd done his required court meetings, and he was doing fine without them. He didn't need a group of people and meetings to keep him sober. He hadn't touched a drop of alcohol for months, and when he felt the urge to drink overtake him, he made sure to get in a long hard run, which seemed to knock the edge off. After all, he wasn't really an alcoholic like the other men. Alcoholics were people who couldn't stop drinking. He'd been able to stop drinking all on his own.

"No problem. Keep us in mind," Coach said. "We'd love to have you on the team."

Sawyer nodded and hustled toward the New Leaf Sewing Shop. It wasn't that he didn't see the value in AA meetings, for some people. But he'd never depend on anything or anyone. He preferred to solve things on his own.

Sawyer pulled open the shop door and crashed into Tyler, who scooted across the slick linoleum shop floor. Strawberry pie crumbs spewed from his plate onto the floor.

"Mm ..." he said, forking a fistful into his mouth. "This is the best Mom's made so far. I hope this competition keeps up all summer."

Sawyer eyed the thick-crusted piece of pie. He hadn't gotten into the pie-eating contest yet, but his stomach rumbled, and he thought he might enjoy it. "Got any more of that?"

"Back table." Tyler winked at him. "Come see my project. The sewing machine is pretty cool, and I'm making a denim tool belt. Maybe one day I can work with you."

"I can always use a hand," Sawyer said, and smiled. When he was Tyler's age, he had enjoyed helping his dad build the dormer on their home. Dad worked on it every weekend, and Sawyer loved learning how things fit together. Bryan and Adam hadn't ever taken much interest in the remodel of their home, and that lack of interest had given him the rare luxury of being able to spend time alone with Dad. In those moments, it seemed Dad didn't expect him to be anything but who he was—his son. Sawyer's chest contracted. If only it had stayed that way all the time.

Sawyer followed Tyler to the back of the room. He strolled to Tyler's station and picked up the denim tool belt. "This is pretty good." Sawyer turned it over. "I bet you could fit at least a couple screwdrivers and a hammer in this thing." He stuck his hands in the large square pockets of the belt.

Sawyer peeked out of the corner of his eye at Katie as she explained to Morgan how to sew a half-inch seam. Emma sat at the sewing machine beside Morgan and bit her lower lip as she threaded a bobbin. Puzzled as to why Lauren was not sitting at the empty sewing machine next to Emma, Sawyer walked over to Lauren, who sat at the far end of the table. He leaned down and whispered, "Are Morgan and Emma coming to your birthday party this afternoon?"

"No." Lauren shook her head adamantly. She didn't look up at him as she tore a seam ripper through a line of seams in her bag with one strong motion.

Sawyer eyed the two giggling girls and frowned. "They're not coming to your party?" Morgan and Emma had been friends with Lauren since preschool. They'd been to all of Lauren's birthday parties.

"They don't like birthday parties."

Sawyer frowned. "That doesn't seem right." Who didn't like birthday parties? He studied Morgan and Katie as they leaned closer together. Why was Lauren's seat at the opposite end of the table? Why wasn't she set up next to the two girls as they giggled and talked?

Determined to get to the bottom of what was going on with the three girls, Sawyer strode up to Katie. He waited until she finished her instructions and Emma and Morgan began working and then motioned to her. "Can I talk to you a minute?"

"Of course." Katie flushed and motioned to the backroom.

Sawyer stepped to the closed door and pushed it open. Katie followed him.

In the darkened room, Sawyer struggled with the temptation to pull Katie in his arms and steal another kiss, but she quickly yanked on a string, and a small light flooded the work area. Shelves of fabric filled the back wall, along with packages of various sewing machine items. A small wooden desk sat in the middle of the room with baskets filled with what looked like bills. A couple of pieces of pie had been placed on the edges of the desk.

"I'm sorry," Sawyer said, and smiled at her. "I didn't mean to sound so threatening. It's a little problem of mine." He cleared his throat. His nerves seemed to be on overtime, making him doubt everything he did around Katie. He needed to get a grip on himself.

"What's the problem?" Katie's voice tightened into her problem-solving business voice.

"I'm a little worried about Lauren." Sawyer cleared his throat. "Morgan and Emma were invited to her birthday party, but they don't want to come. They've all been friends since kindergarten, and I don't understand what's going on."

"Mm ..." Katie leaned against the small desk and crossed her arms over her chest. "Girl friendships can be hard. I've noticed a tension among them, too."

"Do you have their parents' phone numbers?" Sawyer pulled out his phone and scrolled through his contact list.

"I'm not sure that's the best plan right now." Katie peered out the door of the sewing shop. Morgan and Emma giggled and chatted at one end while Tyler talked to Lauren at the other end of the table.

"No?" Sawyer dropped his phone into his pocket. He trusted Katie's judgment. She'd taken Lauren under her wing a few years ago, and the two spent many hours together working on crafts and cooking. She'd also been a trusted confidante of the Cranberry Bay citizens for years, including his mom when she struggled with retiring from her longtime job as the town librarian. It'd been Katie who suggested she spend mornings volunteering at the school's kindergarten classes reading to the kids and sharing her love for the children's books. But at the same time, Sawyer wanted to solve problems for his daughter like he tackled his business developments. He wanted a plan and steps to take and the problem to be solved. "We should make a plan. Try to figure out how to make the girls friends again."

Katie frowned. "It won't work that way. You can't force friendships."

Sawyer leaned back against the wall, and his shoulders slumped. "I guess I don't understand. I grew up with brothers. We fought. We argued. But at the end of the day, everyone got along."

Katie touched his arm gently. "I'm not sure what the problem is with the girls. But I'll try and see if I can get to the bottom of it, okay?"

Sawyer exhaled. "It's been hard for Lauren not having a mom. My family tries to make up for it, but it's not the same. Mother's Day at school is a big deal. The kids grow plants and flowers, and they have a brunch for the moms. My mom often goes, but she still comes home from school wiped out."

Katie nodded. "I know what she feels. After my mom died, the holidays never felt the same. It was like there was always something missing. I'd try to cook her favorite food or recipe, but I'd much rather just have her here with me."

"You're a great help to her," Sawyer paused. "Us."

Katie flushed. "I enjoy spending time with Lauren and …"

Sawyer's heart fluttered, and his stomach dove into his feet. He shuffled them and shifted his gaze away from Katie. A long row of binders lay alongside a table. Above a small desk hung a small, framed photo of Katie standing with her mom. Sawyer stepped closer and peered at the picture. Katie looked to be about sixteen. She wore her hair pulled back in a ponytail and a red T-shirt and jeans. Her mom, who wore a long, colorful skirt and blouse, had her arm looped with Katie's. Behind them stood a large sign, "Scraps and Pieces Scrapbooking."

"Mom loved spending time at the scrapbook shop." Sawyer tapped his finger on the desk and stared at the picture. How could he have forgotten how his mom had spent hours creating elaborate scrapbooks of his baseball games? Pictures of his childhood framed with cheery borders and construction paper. She'd created a scrapbook for each of the Shuster children's school years, but it'd been his that had been the thickest with awards, ribbons, and achievements. After a long day, Mom could often be found with her cup of tea as she worked at a small table in the basement recording her children's childhoods. Sawyer swallowed. How many basements and attics in Cranberry Bay had scrapbooks from Katie's mom's store? How many women had pored over the creation of the books while they poured out their family stories?

"That's Mom and me when she became the owner of the shop," Katie said and stepped up beside him. Her side lightly brushed against him. "She loved her shop. After she died, I hated to change the store over from a scrapbook shop to a sewing shop, but I couldn't keep the scrapbook shop going. People weren't that interested any more in cutting and pasting, and the classes had been all Mom's love."

Sawyer eyed the photo and rubbed his hand over his forehead. His head pounded with a pulsing headache. This was the shop Katie loved. She had built the store with her mom. This wasn't just a place to go for a job. Katie's history lived and breathed in this store. Something inside him pressed against his chest. He took a few deep breaths and closed his eyes.

Katie touched his arm. "I've got to get back before mayhem takes over."

Sawyer nodded and shut the small door beside him. He couldn't shake the heavy feeling in his chest. Katie's store was more than business to her, and he had threatened it by bringing in Craft Mart. Sawyer's stomach churned.

Chapter Eleven

Katie shifted the small blue-and-white bag to her left hand as she headed up the hill toward the Shuster's house. She would never dream of missing Lauren's birthday party and couldn't wait to see the young girl's reaction when she opened her gift. Katie's sandals clicked on the sidewalk as her feelings for Sawyer bubbled like a foamy bath. The way his lips moved against hers, the way he had held her in the gazebo, and the way she had felt so warm in his arms. But this was the man who with one decision had brought in a store that would destroy her business. The man who had no heart for the small-town soul of Cranberry Bay. The man whose every move was driven purely by his needs. She could not allow her guard to drop because of one kiss. She had to keep her wits about her. She was attending Lauren's birthday party because the young girl had asked her to be there. No other reason.

Determined, Katie quickened her step up the hill until she reached the two-story Shuster home. Cars lined the driveway, and Katie recognized Sawyer's, Rylee's, and Lisa's parked alongside each other. Lauren's three-speed bike lay against the side of the house, and her white basket filled with Ivy's fake daisy flowers tilted sideways. The heavy black front door stood open. Flowers pots of red, white, and blue geraniums filled each step. A festive summer flag with sunflowers flew from a white post on the side post of the porch. Laughter spilled from the home.

Katie took a deep breath and rang the doorbell.

"Katie!" Rebecca opened the screen door. She wiped her hands on a red-and-white gingham apron. "Come in, dear," she said, smiling at her. "Everyone is in the backyard."

Katie nodded and swallowed hard. She had only been to the Shuster home a few times. As a teen, Katie had often walked past the welcoming home on her way to her mom's store after a late afternoon at school. In the early fall evenings, the lights inside the home glowed with warmth. Katie often wondered what it would be like to be a family with so much love and laughter pouring from the windows.

Now, she followed Rebecca through the warm and cozy living room. Family pictures lined both the mantel of the fireplace and the wall above the dining room table. Rylee had told the sewing circle about Thanksgiving dinner and how they all shared something they were grateful for at the large oak table. Katie tried to imagine what it would be like to sit at the large table full of family, laughter, and love. She spent Thanksgivings serving dinner at the community hall. She loved spooning out thick gravy over turkey for the local folks who didn't have the ability to buy and cook their own dinner. It took her mind off the empty house that awaited her afterward.

"Everyone is out in the back." Rebecca turned and smiled at Katie.

Katie nodded as she wandered through the small kitchen filled with red and yellow helium balloons. Her stomach jumped with nerves as she steeled herself to walk into the warm family gathering. There was always a small part of her that ached around the Shuster clan. A part of her that wanted family and home so much it hurt, yet they seemed to elude her, first in her own family and then in her short marriage.

Rebecca pushed open the screen door, and Katie followed her. She pushed aside her churning emotions and reminded herself that the day was about Lauren and about enjoying her birthday party.

"Don't cheat!" Lauren's high-pitched voice commanded Maddie and Tyler as they played a game of croquet on the grassy lawn.

Tyler leaned down and hit the ball with his wooden mallet. It rolled toward a small wire arch-shaped stake and stopped inches away. "So close!" Tyler swung his mallet in the air as Maddie reached down and aimed her own red-and-white ball toward the same metal arch. Her ball soared inside and rolled out on the other side. She clapped her hands and smiled at Tyler. "That's the way to do it."

"Lemonade is over here!" Rylee waved to Katie from her seat beside Bryan. Each sprawled on matching wooden Adirondack chairs. Rylee shifted and crossed her ankles. She smoothed her hands over her paisley summer skirt and reached out to place her hand on Bryan's arm in a casual touch.

"We kept Lauren from drinking all of the lemonade," Adam said and chuckled. He sprawled in a straight back chair. His feet stuck out in front of him, and his hair curled around his narrow face.

Sawyer stood beside a cardboard table and arranged packages beside a plate of cupcakes.

Katie took a deep breath and walked toward him. She placed her package on the edge of the table. She was careful to make sure her body did not touch his and ignite any more of the passion stirring within her.

"Why don't you place it beside mine?" Sawyer looked down at her, the warmth in his eyes making the butterflies dance.

Katie dropped her eyes to his lush lips and chiseled chin. She could hardly focus as she picked up the package, and her hand brushed against Sawyer's as he took it from her. Neither moved.

Sawyer's eyes caressed her face and then dropped to her lips, as if he was thinking the same thing she had just been.

Trying to contain her racing emotions and hold herself to together, Katie picked up a small box of candles. Her hands fumbled with the box and shook slightly as she placed a candle in a chocolate cupcake.

"Sasha outdid herself," Katie said, trying to make small talk and keep her emotions at bay.

"Yes." Sawyer nodded. "I'm glad I didn't have to stop at the store and pick up one of the day-old cakes."

"The store cakes are good too," Katie said and stiffened. The day-old cakes had been all her mom could afford for her birthday. Most of the time, they were more than a day old. Sometimes the cakes had the name Sue or Bill scrawled across the top in pink or blue lettering.

"Sure they are," Sawyer continued, unaware of the conflict churning inside her at the memory of her childhood birthday parties. "But Sasha's are the best."

"Yes," Katie nodded and moved the conversation away from cakes. "At least we don't have to eat more pie." She smiled. The pie competition had really taken on a life of its own. Katie and Beth had reverted to setting up small stands, like lemonade stands, at the park and along the bicycle trails with their pies and ballot boxes.

Sawyer touched the top of her hand. "I can finish the rest of the candles. We saved an empty chair for you by Rylee." His voice was deep and low and caressed something inside her.

"Okay. Thank you." Katie's voice felt stuck in her throat, and her legs trembled. It would feel good to sit down. She placed the box of candles on the table and turned toward the chair beside Rylee. Gratefully, she sank down on the edge of her chair. Something in her couldn't quite relax. It seemed to be a part of her for as long as she could remember. The feeling of never being able to be completely comfortable for fear of needing to leave at any minute. It came from years of living with her father and then ex-husband, and she could never quite shake it.

Sawyer stepped behind her. His fingers lightly touched the chair, and she jumped.

"Katie?" Rylee touched her arm. "Are you okay?"

Katie swallowed and nodded. If anyone understood families, it was Rylee. "Of course."

Rylee picked up her hand and squeezed. "Everything is going to be fine," she said under her breath. "Trust me."

Tyler and Lauren clattered onto the patio and dropped their croquet mallets in a heap. Maddie followed and picked up the mallets and leaned them against the side of the porch, out of the way of anyone who might trip over one and fall.

"Is it time for the cupcakes and presents?" Lauren asked Sawyer, her eyes wide as she gazed at the full table.

"Don't you want to eat your cupcake first?" Sawyer raised an eyebrow at her and grinned in a boyish smile that took Katie's breath away. She so rarely saw Sawyer relaxed and at ease the way he was around his family. He had a lot on his plate with running his company, and taking care of Lauren and his large estate. It was good to see him enjoying the day as much as everyone else.

"I've got the cupcakes." Maddie set each cupcake on small yellow vintage tea plates and handed one to each person.

Rylee took the plate Maddie handed out and immediately bit into the soft gooey cake. "Mm....I think I like this better than the pies." She lowered her voice. "Don't tell Sasha."

Katie smiled and took a bite of her cupcake. The sweetness oozed in her mouth and around her tongue. Rylee was right. The cupcakes were better than Sasha's pies.

Lauren set her half-finished cupcake on the patio table beside Lisa and dashed to the present table. "I want to open Katie's gift first."

"Katie?" Sawyer lifted his eyebrows.

Katie nodded. "That's fine with me."

Sawyer lifted Katie's bag from the table and handed it to Lauren. "Careful," he said. "There might be something breakable in there." He winked at Katie.

Lauren grabbed the bag from her dad and pulled out the tissue paper. She tossed it onto the gift table and lifted out a pink gingham apron. "Ohhh …" Lauren squealed. "It's just like Lisa's apron!"

"Look closely." Rebecca refilled Lisa's glass of lemonade. "It's got something more than Lisa's apron."

Lauren held the apron out. She ran her fingers over the lace handkerchief pocket. Katie had stitched the edges with a light pink thread to match the embroidered letter. Small pink flowers trailed along the letter. "This was your mom's. I remember," Lauren said to Katie. "You showed it to me. Her name was Lori, and she had the same first letter as me."

"Yes." Katie nodded. "And look closely."

Lauren pointed to the top edges of the apron and turned to Rebecca. "This is the lace from my mom's wedding dress?"

Rebecca nodded as tears filled her eyes. "Yes. We gave just a small bit to Katie to add to your apron. The apron is a special one to wear to help me serve holiday dinners. It's not to wear in the kitchen to cook like your other one."

"Thank you." Lauren held out the apron to Katie. "Can you help me put it on?"

"Of course," Katie took the gingham fabric and tied it around Lauren. She adjusted the bottom and, when satisfied the apron fit correctly, pulled Lauren into a warm embrace. Lauren's soft form pressed against hers. The little girl who had been brought to her through the shared experience of the death of their mothers filled a small spot in her heart for the daughter she would never have.

"I wish you were my mom," Lauren said quietly.

Tears pooled in Katie's eyes, and she blinked rapidly. She glanced above Lauren to see Sawyer's face soften with emotion, which sent her spiraling into a place that felt deep and dark and yet comforting and like home.

Chapter Twelve

Sawyer grabbed a red-and-white striped towel from a small hook on a cabinet. He picked up a glass from the counter and glanced out the window above the sink. In the small backyard, Katie tapped her croquet mallet on a yellow-striped ball, and it rolled into a wire wicket. Beside her, Lauren frowned, Maddie shrugged, and Tyler slapped his hands together in a high five. Katie pumped her arm in the air and twirled around as if she was no older than the children playing the game. A broad smile broke across Sawyer's face. If he weren't helping his mom with the dishes, he'd be out there playing the game himself. He always loved a good round of croquet and had been the family champion as a child.

At the sink, his mom dunked another glass into the hot soapy water. "It's nice to have Katie at the party. Lauren really enjoys being with her."

"Yes." Sawyer placed a dried glass in the cabinet above the counter. "Lauren and Katie have really bonded." He cleared his throat.

Rebecca peered at her son. "Only Lauren and Katie?"

Sawyer's ears felt hot, and he busied himself with drying. "Katie and I have fought each other for years over development in this town." He struggled to push away the memory of holding her close in the gazebo and kissing her.

"Yes," his mom said, her words slow and measured. "The two of you are very headstrong about how development should be done in Cranberry Bay." She touched Sawyer's arm. "But I think you actually fight for the same thing."

"We do?" Sawyer raised an eyebrow at his mom. He'd always appreciated her wisdom and often sought her out for advice on business matters. But this seemed a little farfetched. He and Katie did not fight on the same team for Cranberry Bay.

"You both love Cranberry Bay," Rebecca said.

"Mm ..." Sawyer leaned against the counter and crossed his arms in front of his chest. Was his mom right? Did he love Cranberry Bay? He'd always thought of it as the town where he grew up. He'd returned because Ginger had wanted to settle down in the small town. She had said it was a better place to raise children then a large metropolitan area like Seattle or Portland.

And it was true. After Ginger died, he had needed the support of his family to help with Lauren. But he'd always believed he'd ended up in Cranberry Bay because of Ginger and not his own desire to be in the small town. Hadn't he once wanted to live in a condo in Portland in the Pearl District? Of course, Ginger persuaded him to let that go and move to Cranberry Bay to start their family, something he had happily agreed to. He had easily transferred his skills to the small coastal towns and quickly built a name for himself. He believed bringing new development to Cranberry Bay was helping to carve out economic security for the small town.

But did he love the town? Sawyer's heart contracted. He hadn't allowed himself to love anyone or anything since Ginger died. It was too dangerous to put your heart on the line for anyone or anything, including small towns, and risk the pain of losing whom or what you loved.

Suddenly, voices filled the small kitchen and drowned out Sawyer's thoughts as Lisa pulled open the screen door, and Maddie, Lauren, and Tyler tumbled inside behind her.

"The party was great." Lisa hugged Rebecca. "But Maddie and I are going to head out, and I'm going to take Tyler home. Lauren wants to ride with us, if that's okay with you?" Lisa turned to Sawyer.

"No problem." Sawyer wiped the counter dry and replaced the towel on the hook. He turned and crashed into Katie, who carried a large basket filled with Lauren's gifts. She had stepped in behind the boisterous group and now took a step back.

Her cheeks flushed pink. "I'll set this in the car?"

"I've got it." Sawyer took the basket from Katie's hands. Their fingers touched, and a jolt of electricity shot through him. He gazed down at her full lips before his eyes trailed upward to meet hers. "Do you want a ride home?"

"That would be great." Katie said and turned quickly to Rebecca. "Thank you so much. I had a great time."

"You are very welcome, dear." Rebecca wrapped her arms around Katie and pulled her into an embrace. Above Katie's head, she winked at her son.

Sawyer shook his head, but a smile broke across his face before he could stop it.

Katie turned and, without looking back at Sawyer, headed for the front door. Sawyer hurried to follow her out the door and onto the driveway. He quickly stepped around her and opened the truck door for her. He took the basket of gifts and set it carefully in the backseat and then hustled around to the driver's side. His heart pounded just a little harder, and he tried to convince himself it was only his quick movements getting settled that caused his breathing to sound just a little bit more shallow than usual. He pushed away the fact that he ran five miles a day and walking around his truck shouldn't make his breath short or his heart pound.

Inside the truck, Sawyer inserted his keys, and the diesel engine roared to life. Sawyer couldn't resist giving the gas a little pressure as it fired up under his foot.

Ignoring his attempts at bravado, Katie rolled down her window and waved to Rylee and Bryan as they headed to her car, which was parked in front of Sawyer's.

"Whoa, brother! Easy!" Bryan shook his head at him.

Sawyer grinned. He felt like he was seventeen. There was something about being around Katie that brought out a side of him he had long forgotten. A playful, boyish youth he'd long ago pushed away. He waved at Bryan and Rylee and pulled out of the driveway, guiding the truck down the street and toward the edge of town.

He glanced at Katie. "I'm glad you came to Lauren's party. I hope we didn't scare you with our boisterous family fun." Sawyer chuckled. The Shuster family did have a way of overwhelming people. Bryan had brought more than one girl home to meet the family whom they never saw again after the gathering. Luckily, Rylee had never had a problem with them, and her return ten years after she and Bryan first fell in love seemed like a long-lost family member finally coming home for good.

"The Shuster clan is wonderful," Katie said. She ran her fingers over the window ledge. "I miss having a family." Her voice cracked.

Sawyer gazed at her. "Is everything okay?" He reached out and placed his hand on top of hers.

Katie nodded but tightened her lips.

"You can tell me if someone said something to upset you." He gripped the steering wheel a little tighter. His brothers could sometimes cross the line, especially Bryan, who wasn't always known for his tact. Although Sawyer hadn't seen that happen very often in recent years. Especially since Rylee had returned to Cranberry Bay, and they had become engaged. But that didn't mean Bryan hadn't said something that upset Katie.

"Oh, no," Katie said. "It's not that at all. Everyone was wonderful. It's just …"

Sawyer waited. His heart thudded against his chest. He felt a strong urge to protect Katie from anything that might harm her.

"It's just sometimes when I'm with a family that is as wonderful as the Shusters, I realize how much I have missed of my own." Her voice echoed with sadness and longing.

"Well," Sawyer said, hoping to take away Katie's sadness. "We have our moments. It can get pretty chaotic sometimes." Sawyer turned onto the small highway leading out to the farmland of Cranberry Bay. "We once tried to take a family vacation together, and it ended up with Bryan at the hospital for a broken arm and Adam sick as a dog over something he tried to eat in the woods. Lisa got a crush on some guy in the next campsite and was heartbroken when his girlfriend showed up. She spent the rest of the trip in tears. I don't know who was the happiest to have the whole thing end. It was a long time before we took another family camping trip."

"But that's what makes it great," Katie said, her voice filled with intensity. "All of that shared history together. The times you've argued, made-up, and laughed together. It's what a family is supposed to be."

"What about your family?" Sawyer asked. "You must have some great memories with your aunt and uncle and mom? Birthday parties? Holidays?"

Katie shook her head. "My aunt and uncle didn't want Mom and me living with them. They took us in because we had nowhere else to go." Katie turned away from him and stared out the passenger window. "We never made a big deal of birthdays or holidays. Mom couldn't afford gifts, and my aunt and uncle didn't want parties at the farm. They said it was a working farm, not a place to have frivolous things like parties."

"I'm sorry," Sawyer touched her arm. "I didn't realize …" He stopped. He was beginning to see there was a lot he didn't realize about Katie. Ginger's family had been like his;

although not all in Cranberry Bay, they lived close enough in Portland and Eugene to be able to share holidays and special events together. He'd never really taken the time to stop and think that there were people around him who didn't have so much family support. Was this why Cranberry Bay was so important to Katie? Did she see Cranberry Bay as family? Was this why so many people who lived and worked in Cranberry Bay fought to save the small town? Because it was family?

Sawyer peeked at Katie as he turned into the long gravel driveway. The moonlight streamed onto her small form beside him. He wanted to reach out and pull her close to him and whisper that nothing would ever hurt her again.

But his insides tightened. He'd made those same promises once. He'd promised Ginger that he would protect and shelter her from every storm, and in the end, he hadn't been able to protect her from the storm that took her life. He hadn't even been able to be there for her in those final months, too caught up in his own grief and drinking to be there for the woman he had pledged to love in sickness and in health. He had no business making promises to Katie. He didn't trust himself to offer her the protection she deserved. But his heart contracted. Something in him still wanted to protect Katie. He wanted to hold the woman sitting beside him and tell her it would all be okay. She'd never have to hurt for family again.

Sawyer punched the garage door opener attached to the sun visor above the windshield with a little more force than necessary and waited as the heavy door slid open before he pulled in alongside the black Studebaker truck. Katie slipped out while he reached into the backseat and lifted out the baskets of presents. Sawyer stepped around the truck and stopped.

Katie stood alongside the Studebaker. She ran her hand over the shiny black side. "I remember the July Fourth parades. Your family always seemed so happy riding in the back of the truck and tossing out candy to the kids."

"Dad loved those parades." Sawyer stepped up beside her. His voice deepened. "He worked on shining the truck for weeks beforehand. Mom and Lisa made sure we never ran out of candy." He smiled. "Although Bryan, Adam, and I ate an awful lot of it along the parade route."

"Do you take the truck out?" Katie turned to him. "There are a lot of antique car shows up and down the coast all summer."

"No." Sawyer stiffened. His voice hardened. "I didn't want the truck. But Mom insisted."

You didn't want to inherit your dad's truck?" Katie frowned.

"Everyone in town loved Dad. But they didn't live with him." Sawyer's gut clenched. He had wanted nothing more than Dad's love. He had believed that by excelling at sports and school, Dad would love him. That quest had sent him on an eternal chase for perfection. When he couldn't live up to Dad's expectations, he had discovered sneaking a few shots of Dad's bourbon dispelled all the feelings he had about not being good enough. It soon became easy to take a shot anytime those doubts and fears inside him surfaced. He learned how to convince the older kids on his sports teams who were back from college to buy him alcohol, which he hid in his room. By the time he turned twenty-one, nightly drinks of bourbon on the rocks had become a habit, and being of age, he no longer had to worry about how to get the alcohol. Unlike his friends, he never drank beer and, instead, chose the hard alcohol as it was easier and faster to get the high he craved. Everyone turned a blind eye to his drinking as long as he continued to succeed.

Katie nodded at him. "I know what you mean."

"Bryan chose to go in the opposite direction of Dad's demands and be a free spirit, something which drove Dad crazy. Adam chose to escape into the woods."

"And you?" Katie's soft voice caressed his insides.

"I did what Dad wanted me to do," Sawyer said. "I played on the sports teams. I excelled at school. I thought if I did the right thing long enough, Dad would love me."

Sawyer crossed his arms over his chest.

Katie stepped closer to him. Her presence was comforting and supportive.

"The morning Dad died, we had a fight. He hadn't shown up at my championship basketball game, and I was upset. It seemed that every time I would land in a top spot, Dad would have something else to do, and it was usually helping someone else. That day, after the game, I headed for the back bleachers with some older guys. Someone got a six-pack, and we sat around and drank it. We figured no one would find out, and if someone did see us, they'd turn a blind eye because we were the town's stellar athletes."

He didn't tell Katie they had spent a lot of time that day laughing at Coach and the silly AA slogans he brought to team practices. Years later, almost every single one of those boys he had drunk with that first night had landed in either rehab or AA themselves.

"I heard the sirens on the way home, and, by the time I got up the hill, the ambulance was at our house. The beer had gone to my head, but I quickly sobered up when I walked in the door and saw Dad on the ground with a paramedic. I was too late." Sawyer's voice cracked.

"And you never got to say good-bye," Katie's soft voice said.

Sawyer shook his head. "No." He remembered the night of Dad's death like it was yesterday. He discovered how powerful drinking could be. That night showed him how alcohol could take away all the pain. It showed him the feeling of being so out of control he couldn't think or feel anything. It showed him how he could numb himself into complete oblivion and wake up the next morning and not remember anything. It was a pattern that had lasted for years. Every time he couldn't deal with something, he reached for the bottle.

Katie reached over and linked her fingers with his. "I'm sorry."

Sawyer nodded. The tears he'd left unshed choked in his throat. There was nothing he could do to ever get that moment back with Dad. But something inside him lifted. He hadn't shared the story of how he felt about Dad's death with anyone. And it had felt so natural. So right to share it with Katie. She hadn't judged him or told him not to feel it. She'd just listened in that quiet, calm way of hers.

Before Sawyer could thank her, a car door slammed outside. Lauren's, Lisa's, and Maddie's voices rose and fell as Lauren headed into the large house and Lisa and Maddie walked to the carriage house across the way from the driveway.

"I should go." Katie unlinked her hand from Sawyer's. "Lauren will want to spend time with you and eat those leftover cupcakes." Katie smiled.

"Katie," Sawyer's voice filled with emotion as he looked down at her. "Thank you for being here."

Katie nodded. Her eyes brightened as she touched his arm briefly before she slipped out the garage's side door. Sawyer stared after her, emotions filling him with something that both exhilarated him and scared him. No matter how much he worked to stop it, he was falling in love with Katie.

Chapter Thirteen

The afternoon sun shone on the hand-painted "Summer Vintage Market" sign. Katie took a step away from the ladder perched against the front of the barn.

"Does that look straight?" She eyed the sign.

"It looks great to me." Ivy placed her hands on her hips. "Anyone know what time it is?"

"We've got thirty minutes before the opening." Sasha whisked by on her way to the small booth beside the open doors of the barn. She balanced an old-fashioned metal tray filled with blueberry, raspberry, and apple pies.

"Thirty minutes." Katie shook her head and stared at the large pile of burlap on the registration table. They'd never finish hanging the triangle-shaped burlap streamers for each vendor inside the barn. She wiped a small bead of sweat from her forehead as strong hands gently touched her shoulders and squeezed lightly.

"I've got the parking ready," Sawyer's deep voice said from behind her. "Three dollars a car, no matter how many people."

Katie's shoulders relaxed. She turned to face Sawyer, and as their eyes met, her insides quivered. The attraction between them had gotten harder and harder to fight. Each time she was around him, she felt herself drawn more and more toward him.

"Yes," Katie checked her clipboard. "Three dollars is perfect. Thank you for allowing us to use your field for parking."

"You're welcome." Sawyer touched her arm and gazed into her eyes.

The buzz of the vendors setting up inside the barn faded away, and all she could feel was the heat between them.

Ivy jostled Katie's arm. "Sorry to interrupt, but there's a problem with the Linens and Lace booth." Ivy rolled her eyes and leaned in close. "They need one of the makeshift walls adjusted and say it's falling in on them. Frankly," Ivy said, and lowered her voice. "I think it's because they've decided to display everything they own on the one wall."

"I'll take care of it." Sawyer touched Katie's shoulder lightly.

Katie nodded as Sawyer hustled off toward the far end of the barn.

"Things going well?" Ivy raised her eyebrow and nodded toward Sawyer's retreating back.

"Of course." Katie consulted her clipboard and avoided looking at Ivy. "It's all just business."

"Business?" Ivy said. "Sawyer does not look at you like it's business."

Katie's cheeks flushed pink, and she busied herself with her notes.

"Craft Mart is opening tomorrow." Ivy shook her head. "The coupons have been stuffed in my mailbox all week."

Katie's stomach took a dive. She'd gotten those same coupons in her mailbox. She had pushed them aside because the week had been hectic preparing for the opening weekend of the vintage market. But her stomach churned and clenched. She couldn't avoid the truth. She couldn't avoid the fact that the man she was falling in love with had brought the business to town that would ultimately destroy hers.

"I am so tired of pies," Sasha moaned as she jotted down the coffee and pastry specials on a large sandwich board. "Why did I ever get into this competition?"

"Because," Katie said, smiling, "you love the competition."

"It'll be over soon, right?" Ivy frowned.

"If it weren't for the tie, the competition would have been over." Sasha scribbled furiously. "Both of us agreed to sell pies at the baseball tournament this weekend."

"But you still have to know who is the best, right?" Katie smiled at Sasha.

"Yes," Sasha nodded. "It's up to the market visitors to vote for the best baker." Sasha tossed her head and her ponytail swung across the shoulders of her sundress. She tied a red, white, and blue half-apron around her waist. "As long as Beth doesn't stuff the ballot box, it should be me."

"It will be." Ivy turned to her truck, which she had parked alongside Sasha's booth. She lifted a crate filled with metal jugs, canisters, and other assorted items from the back. "You make the best pies."

"There you go again." Beth strutted up to the open doors of the barn from the parking lot in the grassy field. "Filling her mind with hopeless dreams. She might as well face it. I bake the best pies, and everyone at the market will know it."

Beth's mouth puckered as she placed a large basket on the cardboard table set outside the entrance to the market. She wiped her hands on her khaki slacks and brushed crumbs off her cream blouse.

"Why don't both of you set up your pies on the front table?" Katie said, and smiled at Beth. "I've got a ballot box." She reached under the table and pulled out a colorful cardboard box. Lauren had decorated it with pictures of pies and large lettering. "As people pay their entrance fee, we'll let them have a taste test. You should both receive a lot of votes this way."

"Great idea." Lisa walked out of the barn, carrying a large pink patio chair. She turned to Katie. "I think this would look perfect in front of your trailer."

Katie clapped her hands. "It's darling! I don't know why I didn't see it."

"Because," Ivy said, "it's been crazy around here for the last week with all the last-minute details."

Katie nodded. It had been very hectic. They had to paint the interior walls of the barn and mark everything off for each vendor, along with taking last-minute additions and cancellations, and juggling sales of the Opening Night tickets. The first week of sewing camp had finished, and she'd spent a couple late nights at the shop, preparing for the second week of camp. By the time Katie arrived home in the evening, she'd fallen into a deep sleep, only to be jolted out of bed as the sun rose so she could do the final work on her trailer before heading off to open the shop.

She headed to a large space that spanned the full back wall of the barn. As one of the market sponsors, Cranberry Bay Antiques had bought three full-length spaces, and Ivy maximized all of it. She set up the entire left corner with open trunks filled with antique china sets, while old windows hung on heavy metal chains from the ceiling. Her fake flowers filled everything from old canisters to metal pitchers.

"Everything looks fabulous." Lisa waved her hand toward the barn's wide-open doors. Canvas flag streamers hung above the freshly painted doors. Music pumped from small speakers and filled the barn with festivity and joy. A small line of vans and U-hauls were parked along the edges of the barn, where vendors unloaded painted furniture, racks of vintage clothing, and baskets of odds and ends.

Lisa stood by the entryway and directed each vendor to their space while Rylee checked them in on a large clipboard. Maddie and Lauren worked at the front table and set up a side table filled with items from the sewing camps. Each of them wore a pretty pink-and-yellow vintage apron, and they had tied their hair back with matching ribbons.

Sawyer stepped out of the barn. "I've got everything all squared away," he wiped his hands on his jean shorts.

Katie hoisted the pink chair, but before she could lift it, Sawyer stepped around her. "Let me get that for you. I'm on my way to the entrance of the field parking lot."

Katie flushed as Ivy's eyebrows raised and Sasha's mouth in a small "O."

"Everything came together very well," Katie walked beside Sawyer toward the camper. "Thank you."

"Not a problem," Sawyer said looking down at her and smiling a grin that sent her heart crashing into her ribs.

They reached the trailer, and Sawyer motioned to the space in front of it. "Where do you want this?"

"Over there," Katie nodded to the rug placed in front of the open door. She had placed a white wicker table in the center of the large rug. Daisies filled three mason jars placed inside a wooden box on top of the table. Sawyer set the pink chair beside the table. It fit perfectly.

"I don't think I ever saw the finished product." Sawyer grinned at her.

"Come on in," Katie said, as she stepped into the trailer. Her heart pounded. She should send Sawyer on his way. She should not allow herself to get swept up by his charms. But she couldn't fight the feelings surging inside her.

Sawyer followed Katie up the trailer steps. He whistled softly. "This really came together."

Katie followed Sawyer's gaze. She'd filled the camper table and open cabinets with fabrics from her shop, precut in fat quarters, half-yards and full yards. Old-fashioned silver buttons filled a large glass candy dish and sat on the counter. She had made small tags for the curtains, bedspread, and pillows, hoping people might want to get some consignment work done.

The small stove held a flowered teapot and matching teacups, as if at any minute she or someone else would pour a cup of tea.

Sawyer ran his hands over the paisley fabric on the bench seats. "This looks really great," he said.

"Thanks." Katie moved, so she stood beside him.

Sawyer turned and looked into her eyes. She raised her face to him as his finger lightly trailed down her cheek. Katie didn't move and held his gaze as he lowered his head toward hers.

Before his lips touched hers, a woman stepped out of the small bathroom. She flushed. "I'm sorry to interrupt. I just wanted to get a look around everywhere. The camper is darling."

"Thank you." Katie said and stepped away from Sawyer.

"Did you refurnish the trailer?"

"Yes." Katie ran her hand over the bench. She warmed while remembering how it had felt to sit on the bench beside Sawyer and bandage his hand, the moment their lips almost met, taunting and teasing her about what could happen. She glanced at Sawyer. "But I had some help."

"I would love to have you make a set of cushions for my camper," the woman gushed. "My husband takes it fishing with the boys, and he has ruined the cushions."

"I would love to do the sewing for you," Katie said, as the feeling she'd once loved in high school when she was approached to sew dresses for dances filled her heart. She quickly pulled out a yellow tablet of paper. "I'll need some measurements, and I'll need to know if you'd like me to pick out the fabric, or give you some ideas, or if you have your own."

"Oh," the woman exclaimed. "There are so many colors of fabric. You choose something for me." She leaned closer. "Rick still needs to take the camper out with the boys, so nothing too frilly, but something that I could live with, too."

Katie scrunched up her nose. "I think I know just the thing," she said and smiled.

Sawyer ducked out of the trailer. "I'm going to go see about that parking."

She was grateful for the distraction of working on an order and designing, and not thinking about Sawyer and how every time she was around him, she could melt into him. Or the fact that after he parked cars, he would be headed over to Liberty Bay Square to check on the final stages of the complex.

Five minutes later, Katie had a sheet full of ideas as a large bell rang from the front of the barn. Katie stuck her head out the door. A line of people waited to pay their entrance fees at the front table, and glancing over the field, a line of cars waited to pay their entry fees and park. Ivy announced in a loud voice. "Welcome to the Summer Vintage Market." The nerves jumped in Katie's throat, but at the same time excitement pulsed through her. They were open for business.

"I've got some friends who would also be interested in custom work, too," the woman said. "Can I give them your number?"

"Of course." Katie reached into her purse and pulled out three of her business cards. Quickly she turned them over and scrawled her cell number on the back. "This is the best number to reach me."

For the next three hours, the market's opening evening flew past in a flurry as visitors carted off tables, chairs, water buckets, and windowpanes. Sasha's and Beth's pies flew from the table, and ballots were cast. Lauren and Maddie helped cart out large refurnished pieces to buyer's cars while people lined up to take a peek inside Katie's trailer. By the end of the night, she had a stack of custom orders for everything from custom-designed drapes and cushions to a couple of summer sundresses.

As the evening wound to a close, and the crowd thinned, Katie stuck her head out of the RV and wandered into the barn. She stopped and talked with each vendor, asking them how the market had gone for their business. Everyone chatted excitedly about what a success opening night had been, and how by the end of the weekend no one would have anything left in their booths. A couple of vendors frantically placed calls to restock their goods from their home stores.

"When will there be another market?" A tall woman at one of the booths asked. "This is fabulous. So much better than sitting in our storefronts waiting for business to trickle inside."

"We weren't planning one until Christmas," Katie said.

"Oh no," the vendor exclaimed. "That's too long. We'd love to do one quarterly. How about in the fall?"

"That'd be perfect. All that good Halloween, fall festive things we can do. Where do we sign up? And, let's have another pie contest. Pumpkin, apple."

Beth grinned as she took a bite of her strawberry pie. "I think we can arrange for that."

"Right here." Lisa waved her tablet in the air. "If you'd like to be a part of the fall show, please sign up before you leave tonight."

Katie's heart swelled as she circulated among the vendors in the barn, making sure everyone had what they needed to open tomorrow morning.

"This is a fabulous space," one woman said, eyeing the top of the barn. "Who did you say helped you with this?"

"Sawyer," Katie said. "Sawyer Shuster." His name rolled around in her mouth like candy.

"The developer who built those houses on the slope?"

"Yes," Katie nodded. "I won his services at the school auction, but the barn needed a lot more work than what I'd bid on. He did it all."

"Well," the woman said. "I never would have expected that from Sawyer. Everyone knows he's about the bottom line." She smiled at Katie. "The two of you must have something special together for him to go the extra mile."

Katie flushed. Did they have something special together? But even more importantly, could she trust him if they did?

Chapter Fourteen

Early Saturday afternoon, Sawyer pulled out of Liberty Bay Square. He turned his truck toward town, and his stomach rumbled. He'd installed a couple of family style chain restaurants in the square, but he needed to clear his head. The morning had been a lackluster opening at best. The doorbuster morning sales generated only a mild interest, not the major one he and the merchants hoped. By midmorning, he'd begun to hear a buzz about the "Summer Vintage Market." The early-bird shopping at Katie's barn had yielded excellent finds, according to the chatter from the people who made their way over to Liberty Bay Square.

Sawyer lifted his hand from the steering wheel and ran it through his hair. He'd never dreamed he'd be pitting the newer items and services in his stores against old, rusty garage sale goods. But it wasn't just the vintage market. It was something else. Something that ran deeper and stretched into every store in the square.

He'd had a heated conversation with the manager of the discount wine shop who had been upset to find a local wine tasting was being held at the beach later in the afternoon. No one was buying the discounted bottles in favor of holding out for a special local wine. The coffee shop owner had pulled him aside midmorning to suggest, next time, they should prevent coffee drinks coming into the square from outside shops. Sawyer only shook his head. He would never be able to stop people from shopping at their local stand and buying their favorite drink. He only hoped the deep discounts of opening day would entice people to purchase from the chain stores.

Sawyer's stomach twisted. A few years ago, he would have sailed into this market. But things had changed. Along with the recession had come a new desire for local buying. People wanted to know who made their products in everything from local groceries to wines to art. They wanted the story behind the item and to know their purchase was supporting someone's livelihood. People didn't want to buy from chains that operated from distant places, with employees who had no idea how the stores had started.

Sawyer turned onto Main Street and parked his car in the public lot by the park. He had been wrong in thinking he didn't need local support. If he wanted Liberty Bay Square to succeed, he was going to need local connections to help bridge the vast divide. The question was how to get that support. His reputation wasn't stellar, and even though people had been excited about the fireworks and the park donation, it wasn't enough to entice shopping at chain stores.

He stepped out of his truck and headed across the street to the bakery. Sasha would be at the market, but a festive summer flag waved outside the open front door. It was the Fourth of July weekend, and people spilled onto the coast from every corner of the state. By the looks of the crowds on Main Street, Lisa's promotion of Small Town Main Street for July Fourth had worked.

Sawyer paused outside of Katie's locked store. Unlike Sasha, she didn't have extra hands helping her, but she had left a handwritten sign, with a small map, that instructed people to visit the Summer Vintage Market. Sawyer smiled at the picture of the pink-and-white trailer printed on the flier. Katie had done an amazing job of transforming it. He'd heard her many nights, late into the night, sanding and working on getting the outside ready to paint. Many times he'd offered his help, but she'd waved him away, saying she wanted to do it herself and she enjoyed the work.

The sign on the fabric shop tilted at an angle, and Sawyer straightened it as he walked by.

His eyebrows shot up as he spotted Lauren in front of the bakery with her bike. He had thought she was with his mom for the day, and they were going over to the market later in the afternoon to help out. They'd been at the opening of Liberty Bay Square early that morning, and Lauren had helped hand out balloons. She was dressed in a white pair of shorts and a blue-and-white polka dot shirt, which she'd bought just for the festivities. Her feet were encased in red sandals, and Maddie had helped her paint her toenails with sparkles. Katie sewed red, white, and blue headbands for all of the sewing circle women and Lauren to celebrate the weekend. Sawyer had both smiled and felt sad as his daughter took extra time to tie her hair into her headband and apply a light coat of lip gloss. It would only be a matter of fast years before she'd be spending all her time in the bathroom preparing for dances and proms.

Now, Lauren stood beside her bike on the sidewalk. Her hair had fallen out of her fabric headband and cascaded into her eyes. Dirt stained her shorts, and a large grease smear stretched across the front of her shirt. Sawyer's heart leaped. Had she been hurt? In a fight? Did she fall off her bike? What had happened to cause her to become so disheveled?

Morgan and Emma pressed up against her, their faces scowling and menacing. The girls' voices strengthened in volume, and Sawyer lengthened his stride to reach his daughter and put a stop to whatever was going on.

Before he could reach her, a large box truck barreled down Main Street.

The truck was going too fast for the road. Although it was a major coastal highway, the signs posted on either end of the town instructed drivers to slow to twenty-five. But the truck driver apparently hadn't seen the sign and maintained a speed much higher than was safe for the crowded area. As the truck moved closer, Lauren tossed her leg over her bike, and it wobbled. Sawyer's heart pounded. Morgan stepped toward her, and Lauren turned quickly toward the street, where she careened off the narrow sidewalk and into the road.

"No!" Sawyer hollered. "Lauren!"

Tires squealed, and the screeching cry of Lauren's voice filled the air.

Metal hitting metal caused everything around him to slow in time and come to a stop. Sawyer ran down the sidewalk in a way he hadn't run since his high school days of playing baseball and rounding the full bases.

Lauren's bike lay in a heap beside the truck's tire. A man in dark jeans and a white T-shirt jumped out of the stopped truck. He spoke into his cell phone. His face pale and white. "There's been an accident. A little girl. She's hurt. Please come quickly."

"Lauren." The words choked in Sawyer's throat as he dropped to his knees beside his daughter. She lay alongside her crumpled bike. Thankfully, the bike had taken the brunt of the force of the truck's wheels as she had swerved. She had fallen off moments before the truck hit the bike. Her leg was twisted at an odd triangular angle, and pain was etched across her face.

"Daddy?" Lauren said, her voice weak and frayed.

"I'm here, baby. I'm here." He picked up her hand and threaded his fingers with hers. "Help is on the way. Don't move."

"I don't feel so good," Lauren said. "My leg hurts."

"I know. We're going to get you fixed up. Everything is going to be okay." Sirens wailed as the aid truck pulled up alongside the box truck.

"Sawyer." Jason touched his shoulder. "The paramedics are here and need room. Thankfully we had no other emergencies right now."

Sawyer had never been so grateful for the small town of Cranberry Bay. The fire station and aid cars parked right behind the post office, only one street up from Main Street. He squeezed Lauren's hand as the doors slammed of the aid car. "I'll be right over here. They're going to take you to the hospital."

Lauren squeezed his hand and closed her eyes. "It hurts."

"Yes." Sawyer's chest ached. He felt the darkness creeping in on him. Another scene swirled in his mind. Ginger telling him it hurt as he'd become furious and confronted three nurses in the hallway about increasing her medication, all while being told there was nothing more they could give her and the hurt wouldn't last much longer. He'd never felt so powerless in his life as the woman he loved, the woman he had sworn to protect and cherish, lay before him in pain, and he'd been helpless to do anything to help her.

"I didn't see her." The truck driver sputtered. His eyes widened. "She darted right in front of me. I didn't see her."

"It's not your fault." Jason placed his hand on the man's shoulder. "We'll get a statement from you and send in the police report to your company." He shook his head. "The whole town has gone bike crazy this summer. It hit us all a little off guard. We'll get this situation taken care of, so it won't happen again."

Sawyer's stomach contracted, and he clenched his fists. The guilt raced through him. He had seen the dangers of the road and the bikes a few weeks ago. He had known this could happen. And he'd done nothing about it. He'd become so absorbed in the last-minute details of getting Liberty Bay Square off the ground that he had failed to do the one thing he needed to do—protect his daughter. No matter what he did, he couldn't protect the people he loved. His stomach rolled over as the voice spoke inside his head. One small shot of whiskey and this pain would go away.

"Sawyer?" Jon Schmidt, the ambulance driver said. "We've got her loaded. We'll meet you at the hospital in Angular, okay?"

"Yes." Sawyer nodded curtly. The North Coast operated out of one hospital, and it was thirty minutes up the highway. It'd been a source of contention for the people of Cranberry Bay for years. But nothing changed. There simply wasn't the funding to run a second hospital along this stretch of the coast.

Sawyer strode to his truck as the ambulance's sirens wailed, carrying his daughter down the crowded stretch of highway. He reminded himself that as long as people moved out of the way, they would reach the hospital long before he would. Lauren would be okay. The paramedics had started pain medication and treatment as soon as she'd been lifted into the back of the vehicle.

But would he be okay? Emotions raced through him. He'd almost lost Lauren. If the scene had played out differently. If she hadn't fallen off her bike and let it take the brunt of the force of the truck, she would have been killed. Sawyer swallowed back the pit of fear and tears in his chest. The one person he loved more than anyone else in the world had come within seconds of losing her life. He clenched and unclenched the steering wheel. But even more than that, he'd become so absorbed in his own interests, he had turned a blind eye to what needed to be done to protect his daughter. She careened up and down the sidewalks, on a regular basis, between her grandmother's house and the small shops downtown, which she loved so much.

Slowly, Sawyer maneuvered his truck through the crowds. The cars packed with families, boogie boards, chairs, and umbrellas for a summer day at the beach. He passed Seashore Cove's liquor store and something in him twisted.

Sawyer clutched the steering wheel harder and turned his radio to a country station. He cranked up the music and forced himself to drown out his racing thoughts and feelings.

Twenty-five minutes later, Sawyer pulled into the hospital parking lot and hustled inside the front doors. "My daughter," he said to a lady at the front desk. "Lauren Shuster? She was just admitted."

"Have a seat in the waiting area, sir." A thin, brown-haired woman looked up from her computer screen. "It'll be a little bit. They've got her in the emergency room."

"How long?" Sawyer leaned over the counter and tried to peer into the blue computer screen on the desk.

The woman shielded the monitor with her hand. "We'll let you know. I know you are worried. But your daughter is in good hands. Please, have a seat." Her voice strained on the last words, and Sawyer leaned away from the counter.

"Sorry," he mumbled and turned to walk toward a long wall of floor-to-ceiling windows that overlooked a hilltop dotted with Craftsman-style homes. A long bridge stretched across the water as it reached toward Washington state. A row of plastic chairs lined the windows, and a couple of people flipped through magazines and stared at their cell phones as they waited. He'd spent days in this room during the final months of Ginger's treatment. But he barely remembered it. Instead, he'd so often slipped out to his car and guzzled another shot of whiskey, numbing and deadening the feelings before returning to sit with his work sprawled out in front of him. No one ever mentioned the smell of alcohol on his breath or his glassy eyes as he finally stepped into Ginger's room and stood beside her bedside, looking down at the thin shell of the woman he had loved all his life.

Today, he couldn't sit down. He couldn't hold himself steady long enough to be still. Pacing, he walked back and forth between the windows and the double glass doors. He wanted a drink. There was no two ways about it. He wanted a drink, and he wanted it now. A drink would ease this feeling inside him. A drink would make everything feel better. A drink would make him calmer.

One drink. It wouldn't hurt anything. Just one tiny drink. Something to take away this horrible feeling. This feeling of being so powerless.

Frantically, Sawyer looked around the waiting room. Two snack machines filled with crackers and nutritional fruit and granola bars sat at one end. A gift shop's open door beckoned him at the far right of the waiting room. Stuffed bears, get-well balloons, and flowers filled the small glass window. The gift shop would have something. It didn't matter what it was—beer, wine, or a small bottle of whisky. Anything would do.

Sawyer strode into the shop, his forehead dotted with perspiration and his palms sweated. He headed toward the back wall of water bottles. A bottle of wine. A six-pack of beer. Anything.

"Can I help you, sir?" A young girl wearing a rainbow-colored smock stood at the front counter. Her blonde hair was pulled up in a shiny blue barrette that matched her eyes. She looked to be no more than sixteen.

"Yes." He turned to the girl. "Where do you keep your alcohol?"

The girl shook her head. "We don't keep alcohol here. There is a grocery store three blocks away." She cleared her throat, and her face flushed. "I wouldn't be allowed to sell it to you. I'm underage."

"Thank you." Sawyer nodded curtly and strode out the door. The grocery store was three blocks away. He had plenty of time to grab a bottle of bourbon and pour himself a couple shots. It wouldn't take much. Just something to calm his nerves.

Sawyer hustled past the reception desk. "Be right back," he called over his shoulder. "Please call me on my cell when my daughter is ready to be seen." He didn't wait for the woman's response and hustled out the door and into the parking lot. He hopped into his truck and inserted his keys into the ignition. His hands shook slightly as he checked the rearview mirror. He didn't think about what he was going to do. He couldn't. All he could do was think about how good the relief was going to feel.

Five minutes later, Sawyer stood in front of the bottles of alcohol in the back of the store. Quickly, he picked up a bottle of Scotch and headed to the register. It was only one drink. Only one shot. Just like taking a pill for anxiety, he told himself. He wasn't going back to drinking. But he couldn't get through this without something. No one understood. He had to have this drink. There was no two ways about it.

Sawyer thumped the bottle onto the counter and pulled out a twenty. He didn't look the clerk in the eyes as the change spit out by his side and he pocketed it and took the bagged bottle. He strode toward his truck and the drink he knew would take care of everything. He could feel it already. A slight warming in his stomach. At his side, Sawyer's cell phone buzzed.

Glancing down, he noted the hospital and the message. "Lauren is resting comfortably. She can see you."

Sawyer froze as if he'd been caught in a trance and had just woken up. He stared at the bag in his hand. The bottle burned through to his skin. The urge to drink fizzled and dropped to his feet. He was not going to drink. He was not going to numb himself out. He was going to walk through this moment with his daughter and be there for her. He was not going to drink and show up at his daughter's bedside smelling like liquor. He was going to be there for her as the Dad she had come to know, the sober Dad she had come to love and trust. He was not going to let her down. He was going to prove he could be trustworthy. Sawyer hurled the bottle into a trash can, where it hit with a loud crash as the glass broke. He turned away from the can and slipped into his car and headed back to the hospital, his emotions racing but his mind clear. After Lauren got out of the hospital, it was time to try out some of those AA meetings. He could use a little help staying sober.

Chapter Fifteen

On Wednesday morning, Katie cut a yard from a bolt of pink-and-green striped fabric. The July sun streamed through the shop's open windows and door. After she finished with the measurement, she placed the empty bolt on a cart behind her and wiped a strand of hair from her eyes. A small bead of sweat pooled on her forehead. She'd been at the cutting table for hours, and a line still snaked between the shelves. No one seemed to mind the wait.

Chatter rose in a low hum as people pored over pattern books, discussed sewing techniques, and browsed Katie's list of upcoming late summer and fall classes, which she hoped to hold in the barn's newly renovated upper loft.

"You're going to need to install a bigger counter." Maddie measured a yard of blue-and-white gingham fabric. "You know, the kind they have at Craft Mart." She sliced her scissors through the fabric in a straight line.

"This is so unusual." Katie frowned and dodged Maddie's suggestion. "Even at the holidays, we aren't this busy."

Julie placed six bolts of pink-and-blue baby fabric on the counter. In the back of the shop, Julie's twins played with a yellow dollhouse in what Katie had designated a children's corner. Julie wore a blue maternity smock over a pair of light paisley shorts. Her painted pink toenails stuck out of gold sandals.

"We'd rather buy from you then that giant superstore monstrosity." Julie patted her round stomach. "I'd like my new little one wrapped in a warm snuggly from your shop."

"You've been so generous with your time. Staying open late, answering all our questions about sewing and fabric. That's not something Craft Mart offers," Missy Steidel, chief of police's wife, shifted her three bolts of Christmas fabric from one arm to the other and reached up to adjust the thick strap on her green sundress.

"But the prices." Katie glanced up at her loyal customers. "And the coupons?" There was no way a small store like hers could ever match the discounts given by the superstores. "Don't you want to get a deal?"

"It's just a few dollars." Julie waved away Katie's protests with the flick of her wrist.

Katie eyed the crowded shop. Julie may not have to worry about a few dollars, but over half of the women standing in the line were on limited incomes of Social Security and small retirement funds. How could they not love coupons at Craft Mart? Instead of being able to afford one yard of fabric, the coupons gave them the freedom to buy two or three yards. Katie wiped another band of sweat off her forehead. She didn't have time to think about it right now as the line grew, and another three women she didn't recognize entered the shop.

The day raced by, and by the time Katie closed the register, her back ached, her feet were sore, and she couldn't measure another bolt of fabric. The shop looked like a cyclone had hit. Fabric bolts were piled behind the cutting counter and tossed haphazardly on every shelf. The button box had been half-emptied, and a large number of the summer skirt, dress, and bag patterns purchased. The entire shelf of holiday fabric was empty, as were most of the soft flannels for babies. It would take weeks to restock everything.

Katie thumbed through the stack of receipts. The totals were higher than she'd ever seen—even higher than the weekend of holiday sales after Christmas. Everything had been sold, including a couple of sewing and embroidery machines, which she had special ordered. She stood and walked to the backroom where she filled a small pot with hot water. Katie opened the large filing cabinet and pulled out a thick manila file. As the water came to a boil on a small warming plate, she flipped through the papers in the file.

She fingered and reread the first lease her mom had signed. She remembered the day as if it was yesterday. Both of them so excited and celebrating their moment of declaring their own lives with a thick slice of chocolate cake. Katie set the lease aside and picked up the paperwork for the first sale of scrapbook paper. She'd placed her own first sale of fabric directly under the first sale of her mother's shop. Katie turned over the papers and read the transfer of the shop to her name and her current lease. She scanned the lease and double-checked the date for what she had known to be true—her lease ended on the last day of July.

If she was going to make a move, now was the time. Otherwise, she'd have to sign another year's lease, and who knew what state her shop would be in after the holiday season with Craft Mart down the road. Katie's stomach turned over. The last thing she wanted to do was sell the shop her mom had loved and given to her. But what choice did she have? If she didn't act now, she'd go into bankruptcy and never have a chance at restarting any business. If she left now, she would be able to walk out with cash funds and begin refocusing her business.

The kettle hummed as she poured hot water over a chamomile tea bag. Katie carried her mug and lease to the front of the shop. The quiet in the store soothed her as the bell above the front door tinkled and Ivy stepped inside.

"Whoa!" she said. "It looks like you had a going-out-of-business sale."

Katie set the lease face down on the counter. "Do you know what is going on?" She drank a sip of her tea.

Ivy shrugged but a smile crept along the edges of her mouth as she strolled past the jumbled patterns. She stopped and picked up a couple of patterns, which lay scattered on top of the cabinet. "People are even buying these patterns at full price?"

"Yes." Katie shifted her warm cup between her hands. "I tried to tell them that Craft Mart would have discounted patterns plus run dollar-coupon specials, but no one listened."

"People don't want to see you go out of business." Ivy sank onto the stool at the counter opposite Katie. Her long braid hung down the back of a pink T-shirt tucked into denim shorts. Her red painted toenails matched her red sandals. Her own store had been doing great since the summer started. There was a renewed interest in repurposing items, and every day customers carried old treasures out the door with glowing faces.

"But how long can they keep this up?" Katie ran her hand over the top of the counter. "Everyone has enough fabric to make three years of holiday and birthday gifts."

"I guess they won't need to go to Craft Mart." Ivy said. "Maybe they want to put them out of business." She chuckled.

"I can't keep asking people to pay full price who are on limited incomes." Katie fingered the corners of the lease in front of her and frowned.

"You're not thinking of closing?" Ivy placed her hands on the edge of the counter and leaned forward.

"At the vintage market, I received a stack of requests for consignment items," Katie said. "If I open a consignment business, I can do what I've always loved to do, which is sew for people." The excitement bubbled inside her at the idea she'd been turning over in her head for weeks. "I'll still teach my classes in the barn. I can run even more camps and classes than I could in the shop. I'll start by having some sewing classes for adults who want to learn to sew this fall."

"But it was your mom's store." Ivy placed her hand on her heart. "How can you give it up?"

"I know," Katie said, as a lump formed in her throat. She had spent so many hours in this shop. First as a teenager helping her mom as they struggled to rebuild their lives in Cranberry Bay and then as an owner as she took her place in the midst of Cranberry Bay's business district and spearheaded community projects. "But I think this is what Mom would want me to do. She wouldn't want to see the store go bankrupt."

But it was more than that and a large pit of fear filled her stomach. She lowered her voice. "Mom always said we stayed too long with Dad. She kept hoping he would change. Every time Dad would get better and stop drinking and the violence would stop, Mom would say we'd turned a corner. But something always happen to set Dad off again." Katie's stomach churned. She'd done the same thing with her first husband, Marc. She had believed that he would get better. She believed he would kick his drug habit and go back to being the person she had once known. But he hadn't been able to. The drugs had been too strong for him, just like the alcohol with her Dad.

"You don't want to give the store a little longer?" Ivy said. "I hear the opening of Liberty Bay Square didn't go well at all. Maybe they'll close."

"No." Katie shook her head. "The Liberty Bay Square stores are national stores. It doesn't matter if one of them has to close. They can absorb the costs. I can't." She thumped the counter. "But, even more. I don't want to believe in false hopes. I want to pull out while there's a chance to make something new and not have to recover my debts." She swallowed. "I don't want to trust something that isn't trustworthy."

Ivy peered at her. "It's more than your store, isn't it?"

"What do you mean?" Katie raised her head and looked at her best friend.

"Sawyer," Ivy said simply. "You don't know if you can trust him."

Katie exhaled. She wanted to trust Sawyer. She loved being with him. She loved how it felt to be in his arms. She loved spending time with him and working on projects, the conversation flowing effortlessly as they joked and chatted together. But could she trust him? On one hand, he seemed to have turned over something new with his involvement with Cranberry Bay and the donation of the land to the parks department. But how did she know that wasn't all a selfish guise for his own interests? He'd brought Craft Mart to town with a shrug of his shoulders, saying it was business. But for her, it wasn't business. Her career was an outpouring of her soul. How could she trust him with her heart?

The store bell chimed as Lisa opened the front door and Rylee followed her into the shop. Both of them carried bags filled with towels and each wore a large sun hat. Their faces were pinked by a day at the beach in the sun and wind. Rylee had gone to check on one of her projects at the beach and encouraged Lisa to come along to look for a job. By the looks of the two of them, the job search hadn't happened, but it'd been a relaxing day in the sand and sun.

"What happened here?" Lisa dropped her bag on the counter.

Katie smiled and shook her head. "A going-out-of-business sale."

"Going out of business?" Rylee's eyes widened as she twirled around the disheveled shop. "You're not leaving Cranberry Bay?"

"No." Katie shook her head. "But I am closing the store."

Rylee pulled out the second stool at the counter and sat down facing Katie. "I'm all ears."

"I could use your ears," Katie said. "You have a great sense for business, and you can tell me if you think this might work."

Katie grabbed a large tablet of paper from below the counter and outlined her thoughts about sewing on consignment, and holding classes and workshops in the barn. When she finished, no one said anything. Katie's heart beat faster as she waited for verification from her best friends. She didn't think it was a crazy idea, but she trusted her friends to tell her if it was.

Suddenly, Ivy hopped from her stool and clapped. "Great job, Katie. I think you've got a stellar business plan. You can be so much more use to people without the shop."

In unison, the other women broke into heartfelt clapping and cheers.

Katie flushed. "I'm so glad you think it will work. Business isn't always brisk, and it always feels like there's so much more I could be doing. I think this will allow me to expand in ways I hadn't planned, plus I won't have the overhead of running and leasing a building."

Rylee dug into her beach bag and pulled out her cell phone. Her eyes gleamed.

"What are you doing?" Katie asked.

"I'm calling Bryan," Rylee said. "He's had an interest in a bike shop on Main Street, and I think your store would be perfect. I want to get the information to him, so he can start working on it. We don't want empty storefronts on Main Street in the height of the summer."

Katie smiled. Rylee's head for business served not only her, but also her fiancé and the town.

"Oh, Katie, Ivy moaned. "Main Street will not be the same without you."

Katie's heart turned over. She would miss the daily and sometimes more than daily conversations she had with Ivy. The times they popped into each other's shops while one or the other ran an errand. The times they worked together on specials and sales, hoping to attract new people.

"I'll miss you too." She leaned over and embraced Ivy. "But I won't be far away, and we can ride our bikes back and forth on the new trails." She would miss the friendship, but she wouldn't be far down the road, and with the new trails, it'd be fun to take a bike ride from her barn workshop to Main Street.

"But there's something else?" Rylee clicked her phone off and peered at Katie.

"No," Katie shook her head. "It's not important."

"Matters of the heart are always important," Ivy said. "Talk."

"It's Sawyer, isn't it?" Lisa stepped up beside Katie and touched her arm.

"Yes," Katie said. Her voice shook. "I didn't mean to fall in love with him. He's always been my enemy. But something happened …"

"Sometimes the hardest thing to do is trust someone with your heart," Rylee said, her voice soft.

Katie nodded. If anyone understood learning to trust someone with their heart, it was Rylee. She'd left Cranberry Bay ten years ago, running from the love of Bryan Shuster, only to return and find that love still waiting for her.

"Sawyer loves you," Ivy said.

Katie shook her head. "Sawyer doesn't love me. Sawyer loves himself."

"You're wrong," Ivy said. "It was Sawyer who set up the flurry for sales in your shop."

"Sawyer?" Katie stared at Ivy. "I thought it was you."

"No," Ivy shook her head. "Sawyer came to me and wanted to help you. He didn't want you to know because he knew you would never take his help."

Katie smiled. Sawyer knew her well.

"Sawyer put the word out. He called each person individually and invited them to shop at your store," Lisa said, and shook her head. "I've seen my brother go after things, but not like what he did with this."

Katie's insides warmed. Sawyer had tried to make things right for her business. He had tried to protect her and what she loved. She had been wrong about him. He wasn't only interested in his interests. He had a heart. A heart for her.

Tears spilled out of Katie's eyes and down her cheeks as she looked at each of the women, the women of her circle. And her heart filled with warmth as she thought of the man whom she loved with all her heart and wasn't afraid to give it to.

Chapter Sixteen

Sawyer shifted the tray with two cups of warm coffee into his left hand. He knocked on the door of Katie's trailer. Lauren had requested he pick up the box of sewing camp projects and fabric still to be sewn. Of course, all of it was a guise for asking Katie to his house for the surprise birthday brunch party he and Lauren had been working on for the last two weeks. The party had given Lauren something to focus on besides her inability to do the summer activities she loved. Once the initial excitement of being able to draw on her cast had subsided, she had spent a lot of time moping around the house and complaining.

When her leg healed, Sawyer knew he would have to allow Lauren back on her bike. He couldn't stop her from doing what she loved. And although the memory would forever be etched in his mind of the squealing brakes and his daughter lying on the ground with her twisted leg, Lauren had already forgotten the incident and kept asking when the cast would came off and she could get on her bike again. Jason had kept his promise. He'd installed new signage outside of town along with flashing lights telling people to slow down. He'd also made sure to place a patrol car near the entrance to stop those who refused to follow the speed limit. Two weeks of constant tickets, and the word had gotten out. Slow down before coming into Cranberry Bay.

"Katie?" Sawyer opened the door and peeked into the small, crowded trailer. Fabric and sewing items lay across the table and bench seats. Boxes filled the bed. It looked like Katie's entire store had blown up inside her trailer.

"Are you looking for me?" Katie asked as she stepped around the side of the trailer. She held a hose in her hand and watered the boxes of red-and-white geraniums. Her hair swirled around her. She wore denim jeans and pink tank top. Her skin had darkened to a summer tan.

"Yes." Flustered, Sawyer stepped down from the steps. He wanted to reach over and kiss Katie. He hadn't seen her in a couple weeks as he'd been busy taking care of Lauren and spending time trying to problem-solve with the merchants of Liberty Bay Square. None of them was happy with the opening day's and first week's sales. More than one had already had their corporate office contact him and threaten to break the lease if he couldn't come up with a plan to get more people into the stores.

"It looks like your whole store is inside the trailer." He smiled at her.

"It is." Katie pushed back a strand of hair from her forehead. She set the hose down in front of her. "You didn't hear?"

"No," Sawyer shook his head. "I've been a little tied up with Liberty Bay Square the last couple weeks. I haven't been over to Main Street."

"I'm closing the store."

"Closing?" Sawyer frowned. "But I thought the sale went well. Why are you closing?"

"The sale was amazing." Katie touched his arm. "Thanks to you."

Sawyer flushed. "They told you. No one was supposed to tell you."

"Ivy can't keep a secret," Katie said and smiled. She didn't remove her hand. "Thank you for your support. I appreciate it."

Sawyer cleared his throat. "You're welcome. I wanted to help you. It was a terrible decision to bring Craft Mart to Liberty Bay Square. I believed it was a business decision." Sawyer gazed at her and his heart filled. "But it wasn't."

The words bubbled to the tip of his tongue. He'd realized Katie's shop was her heart and soul. He had come to see that it wasn't just business with her. She lived and breathed the passion of helping others and supporting Cranberry Bay through her store. But even more than that, he had realized something else. Something far more important. He loved the woman standing in front of him. He didn't want to be bound by the chains of his past any more. He was capable of being the man Katie needed, and he wanted to prove it to her.

Katie took a cup of the coffee, and their fingers touched. "The business has been struggling for a while. I didn't want to tell people because so many depend on having me in the middle of Main Street. But it's time to move on and try a different approach before I lose everything." She smiled at him. "It's just business, remember? How is Liberty Bay Square?"

Sawyer exhaled. "Not good." He drank a long sip of coffee. "People want local. They want the local stories behind what they are buying and are willing to pay extra. I underestimated my market."

"Mm ..." Katie nodded. "There does seem to be a renewed interest in local stores. The Main Street merchants are telling me they are having one of their best seasons ever. We're already planning for the fall vintage market, and it looks like it will be bigger than the summer."

"I need to rethink things at Liberty Bay," Sawyer said. "We really need a consultant, someone who knows the local markets and could help give us ideas." He raised his eyebrow at Katie.

"Oh no," Katie said, waving her hand in front of her face and laughing. "You and I working together would never work. You know we stand on opposite sides of the fence."

"Not this time," Sawyer said and chuckled. "What if I hired you to be the local consultant for Liberty Bay Square?" The words poured out of his mouth. Katie would have the skills he lacked. She would know how to connect the locals to his shops, something he didn't seem able to do.

Katie drank a long sip of her drink. "It could work. I'm not going to be as involved with the Main Street merchants and I could still do my consignment business but also work with you on some new ideas. We could have poetry readings in the coffee shop, encourage the local community sports teams to visit the restaurant with corporate sponsorships." Her eyes glowed with passion and excitement. "It would be a challenge, but I'm up for it."

"Good." Sawyer stood and looked down at her, his eyes warm and gentle. "There's something else, Katie."

Katie gazed up at him. Her eyes soft.

Sawyer took a deep breath. He couldn't deny it any longer. He loved Katie, and he wasn't going to push it away any longer. "I …" His cell phone beeped against the side of his leg and Lauren's text splashed across the screen. "We're ready."

"Business?" Katie asked and pointed at the cell phone.

"No," Sawyer said, shaking his head. He cleared his throat. "I came to see if you wanted to have breakfast with me. It's your birthday, and I don't want you to be alone."

Katie's eyes warmed and softened. "You remembered."

"Of course," Sawyer said, holding out his hand to her. "I remembered."

Katie slipped her hand into Sawyer's and stood in front of him. Neither one of them said a word as he gazed into her eyes and the morning settled around them.

Suddenly Katie broke away from him. "Let me get that box of things for Lauren. She's been bugging me about new fabric and buttons for some project she is working on."

Sawyer nodded as she hurried inside the trailer. In seconds, she had draped a blue cardigan sweater around her shoulders and picked up a box of assorted odd items. As she stepped down the trailer steps, Sawyer took the box from her. He threaded his fingers through hers, and the two walked into the fields bordering their two homes.

"I talked to Morgan and Emma's parents," Sawyer said. "Both of them promised the bullying wouldn't happen again. They are sending both girls to counseling."

"Good," Katie said. "I'm glad. I had a few words with both of their parents after the last session of sewing camp. Both of them want the girls in separate classes. I believe Morgan's family is considering sending her over to the beach elementary school."

As the two reached his patio, Sawyer set the box down and pulled open the French doors. The smell of hickory coffee and baked cinnamon rolls filled the air.

"Is she here yet?" Lauren hobbled into the kitchen from the dining room where she had been spreading a paper "Happy Birthday" tablecloth on the table. The room that, for so long, had been stifling and unused now boasted a thick pile of scones, another of cinnamon rolls, and a steaming bowl of scrambled eggs. A tall pitcher of iced juice sat on the sideboard along with a pot of coffee. The breeze from the open windows floated in and brought a light fresh summer scent of honeysuckle and jasmine.

"Is who here?" Rebecca stepped into the room while Ivy, Sasha, and Lisa trailed behind her, all of their arms full of packages and brightly wrapped presents.

"I need some coffee." Sasha moaned. "I only slept three hours last night."

"Working on your next pie recipe?" Ivy picked up a blue mug and poured coffee before handing it to Sasha.

"I can't believe Beth won." Sasha took a large drink. "I know she stuffed the ballot box."

"You'll get her in the fall." Ivy dropped an arm around Sasha's shoulders. "Your cranberry pie is the best!"

"What are you all doing here?" Katie asked, her voice filled with surprise and delight.

Sawyer stepped forward and placed his arm around her. He cleared his throat. "We are having a birthday party." He picked up Katie's hand and threaded it with his. "For you." The room behind him stilled, and he swallowed.

"Birthday party?" Katie slowly looked around the room. "For me?"

"A birthday party for you." Sawyer reached down and picked up her hand, linking his fingers with hers as the women circled Katie and sang a loud "Happy Birthday."

When the song finished, Sawyer leaned down and softly kissed Katie on the lips. "I love you, and I hope to spend many more birthdays with you. Always."

Katie turned her face to him. Her eyes were bright, and her smile glowed.

Sawyer lowered his lips to hers and very softly kissed the woman he loved.

About the Author

Best-selling author Mindy Hardwick enjoys writing sweet contemporary small-town romance as well as children's books that celebrate art and community in the Pacific Northwest. Her published children's and young adult books include: *Stained Glass Summer*, *Seymour's Secret*, and *Weaving Magic* as well as a digital picture book, *Finders Keepers*. Mindy can often be found walking on the Oregon beaches and dreaming up new story ideas with her cocker spaniel, Stormy. Mindy loves hearing from readers, and you can follow her blog to find out more about the Cranberry Bay series and participate in fun blog hops with great giveaways:

www.mindyhardwick. wordpress.com

Please enjoy an excerpt from the first book in the Cranberry Bay series, *Sweetheart Cottage*:

SWEETHEART COTTAGE

A gust of wind threatened to shove Rylee's car off the Oregon highway and down the steep cliff to the forest below. She tightened her grip on the steering wheel and sang loudly with her favorite country-and-western singer, trying to drown out her increasing fears about the trip to Cranberry Bay.

Rylee slowed to peer at a small blue sign that pointed to a rest stop tucked into the backside of the mountain. She checked the rearview mirror. Her black,-white-and-tan mutt, Raisin, stood on a threadbare towel in the backseat. He whined and pressed his nose to the glass. Rylee turned on her left blinker and slowed to exit.

"We'll get out of this storm," she said to the dog, more to reassure herself than Raisin. Rylee frowned at the small GPS attached to the dashboard. It hadn't picked up a signal to Cranberry Bay for miles, and she hoped it wasn't broken. She hadn't been back to the small town in ten years, not since she left Bryan. Rylee bit her lower lip and pushed away the thoughts of leaving her childhood sweetheart the morning after he proposed. She tried to focus on driving down the dark and rainy mountain road, where nothing looked the same as she remembered.

A small headache pounding between her eyes, Rylee followed the signs to the rest stop, pulling off the freeway onto a long ramp. She stopped in front of a brown, wood-shingled building. Picnic tables and a path curved down a hill toward a rushing stream. Towering evergreen trees surrounded the open green space. Signs pointed toward men's and women's restrooms. There wasn't another car in the parking lot, but a light glowed from a middle window in the building.

"Okay, bud," Rylee said. "It's going to be wet." She smiled at her faithful companion, who had ridden with her on the hundred-mile trip from Vegas. She didn't doubt Raisin understood rainstorms. She'd found him huddled against a Dumpster in the back alley outside her condo. It hadn't taken much to coax him inside; the leftover bite of her turkey sandwich was enough. Raisin became her only confidante as she packed up and sold everything off. Rylee's stomach twisted as she thought about the text she received from her partner and former best friend. Ericka had eloped with Rylee's fiancé and wanted out of their shared business immediately. Rylee was left with nothing but maxed out credit cards and rent on an expensive storefront. Only the letter she received from her grandmother's lawyer had given her any hope.

Rylee opened the car door, and the wind rushed through her short cardigan, thin lace shirt and cropped pants. She blasted the car heater to take away the mountain chill. None of the black pumps, skirts, and thin blouses inside her old, beat-up suitcase would be any warmer. But it didn't matter. She planned a quick sale of her grandmother's place. Once she convinced her gambling father to leave Vegas, something she knew he'd do as soon as he realized she was leaving him, she'd be on her way to San Diego to restart her life.

Rylee shivered and pulled her black cardigan tighter. Rain dripped against the side of her face as she stepped out of the car. A gust of wind blew strands of her hair against her mouth, and she pushed them aside and opened the backdoor. Rylee clipped on a leash and guided Raisin out of the car. The wind tossed Raisin's ears as he shook-off of the last five hours of travel. The trees above her head swayed, and Rylee quickly stepped away. A large branch could easily damage her car or hurt her.

Rylee hurried to the warmly lit building. She stepped under the covered porch. A coffee pot sat on a ledge beside a basket of napkins. A couple of dollar bills were stuffed inside a yellow coffee cup plastered with a black smiley face. A small handwritten sign said: "Donations Accepted."

"Cup of coffee, my dear?" A round-faced woman with deep-set blue eyes peered back at her from the other side of an open glass window. A basket of sewing yarns, threads, and measuring tapes was perched by her feet, and an old pair of jeans rested across her lap.

"Yes, please." Rylee reached in her pocket and pulled out a crumpled dollar bill. She dropped it in the donation cup and poured a thick stream of rich black coffee into a Styrofoam cup.

"Stormy evening." The woman pushed a plate of white-frosted oatmeal cookies toward Rylee.

Rylee shook her head at the cookies. "No, thank you." She barely had the dollar donation for the coffee. She didn't need cookies too.

"Go on," the woman's soothing voice wrapped around Rylee like a hug. "The chocolate-chip oatmeal cookies are my homemade special."

A deep ache dove through Rylee's chest. Grandma always made cookies for her when she arrived in Cranberry Bay for her summer childhood visits. Peanut-butter, chocolate-chip, and oatmeal cookies waited for her inside a colorful, old-fashioned tin that once belonged to Rylee's Great-Grandma. Rylee made a mental note to find her grandmother's tins. She planned to tuck a few things into her car before everything was marked to sell in the estate sale.

"Thank you." Rylee took a cookie from the tray and bit into it. The sweetness filled her mouth. It tasted exactly like her grandmother's recipe.

"I'm Beth Dawson. I run the coffee program at the rest stop for Cranberry Bay Community Youth. All the donations go toward helping youth attend a local summer camp where they can learn to swim, fish, and enjoy hiking."

"That's nice," Rylee muttered, not wanting to give away her own connections with Cranberry Bay. She was there only to sell her grandmother's house, and then she'd be on her way. Well-meaning strangers only threatened her family's longtime rule of not revealing her father's gambling secret. It was a secret they had kept since her father left town in his twenties, headed to a career as a minor league baseball player. The baseball career never materialized, and her father drifted into a twenty-year addiction with gambling. Years later, still unable to tell the town the truth about their famed hometown hero, Rylee had been driven out of Cranberry Bay and away from Bryan by her father's secret. She didn't need a reminder written on her calendar to remember to keep to herself during this trip.

"Do you have a pen?" Beth asked. "I'll write down the name of the camp. We accept donations all year-round. We're always looking for businesses to sponsor the kids."

Rylee fiddled in her purse for a pen. Once she got to San Diego and secured her job, she'd send a check to cover at least three kids. Giving back was a part of her business plan and something she made sure to include on her yearly goal chart. After all, Cranberry Bay was a town she always enjoyed visiting as a child.

Beth quickly wrote down the name of the camp and a website. "Here you go." Hope filled Beth's eyes. "Please. It's really important to these kids that they have a chance. If there is a business that is looking for a place to donate, we'd love to talk to them. We also love for people to volunteer. That's just

as important as the money donation. Maybe if you have time
..."

Abruptly, Rylee took the pen from Beth. The blue-and-green company emblem plastered to the side of it taunted her with everything she had lost. "I'll keep the camp in mind for a donation."

Tucking the piece of paper in her purse, Rylee walked over to the trash can, where she promptly dumped the pen and all reminders of her former life. Impatiently, she tugged on Raisin's leash and strode back to her car with the dog trotting behind her.

Quickly, she loaded Raisin into the backseat. Rylee slipped into the driver's seat and fiddled with the GPS buttons on her dashboard. The screen remained blank. Rylee frowned and pulled out of the parking lot. It couldn't be that much farther to Cranberry Bay. There should be signs pointing her in the right direction. Rylee breathed in and out. She hoped to arrive to Cranberry Bay before dark.

Rain pounded on the roof and a large semi-truck passed in the other lane. Water sprayed over her windshield as she slowed to avoid hydroplaning into the truck's lane. Rylee peered through the windshield and searched for a road sign telling her she needed to turn off the highway to reach Cranberry Bay. She didn't remember much about the trip when Grandma and Grandpa used to pick her up at the Portland airport. After Mom died, Dad always made sure to send her to Cranberry Bay for the entire summer. Both of them pretended they didn't know Dad would spend the summer in the casinos. She loved those childhood summer days when daylight stretched far into the evening. By the time she was nineteen, she and her childhood sweetheart, Bryan, had declared their love for each other. Even now, her insides warmed as she remembered how he made her feel—loved, cherished, and protected. The night he proposed, she believed everything would finally work out. She would find a way for

Dad to get help for his addiction. He could return to Cranberry Bay and enjoy his life again. But the next morning, everything had crashed when the Vegas police called. She left immediately, knowing she could never leave her father alone in Vegas, and he couldn't return to Cranberry Bay until he was the hometown hero they all remembered and loved. But ten years later, her father was still gambling, Bryan had married someone else, both her grandparents were dead, and she had just lost the only thing she had left in the world—her career.

A blast of wind blew across the highway, and Rylee swerved to avoid missing a small branch. Raisin let out a sharp bark and paced back and forth on the backseat. A small tire light on the dash flashed, and the car bumped with a flat. Rylee cursed and steered toward a small gravel pullout. In the summer, motor homes and slow-moving cars stopped to allow streams of cars pass. Now there was no one on the gravel road. Rylee drove alongside a small trailhead and parked.

Twenty-four hours before she left Vegas, Rylee had traded in her gorgeous black Lexus for an old, four-door car with the large dent on the left side. The dealer told her the used car needed new tires. She had a budget for how long she could make her meager savings account last. New car tires were not in the budget.

Rylee reached over to the passenger seat and fumbled inside her brown leather purse. She'd simply call her emergency roadside assistance number for help. Rylee unzipped her purse and pulled out her phone, only to see the small message in the window: "No service." That explained the GPS problem.

Hold it together, she told herself as panic rose in her chest. She could handle the situation. The enclave of trees must be blocking the reception. She would simply walk back to the rest stop and ask Beth for help. It had to be less than a mile back down the road. She could walk a mile. On her treadmill, she walked at least three miles a day. Of course, it wasn't in the middle of a windstorm, and she always wore her expensive sports shoes during her workouts, not her flimsy open-toed black sandals. But those were just details.

Rylee peered outside the window. She longed for the small blue emergency bag Grandma and Grandpa tucked into the backseat of their car. As a child, Rylee loved to explore the blue bag and check for the white candles, matches, flashlight, extra batteries, flares, granola bars, water jug, and the thick maroon blanket. One summer, she created an entire spreadsheet of the items in the blue bag and gave it to her grandparents. They tucked the paper inside the front pocket for safekeeping.

She pressed her nose to the window. If she walked against the traffic on the left side of the road, she could do it. "Come on, bud," Rylee said to Raisin. "We're going for a little walk."

Rylee stepped out of the car as headlights rounded the bend and splayed into her eyes. She lifted her hand to shield her vision from the glaring lights. A tree branch cracked behind her and landed somewhere close by with a thud. She didn't need her list of goals to tell her she had to get out of here. Fast.

The small truck slowed, and Rylee's heart pounded. The only person who expected her was her grandparents' lawyer, and her appointment was on Monday morning. There wasn't a person in Vegas who cared where she was, and, except for Beth Dawson, she hadn't talked to anyone in days. By the time someone realized she was missing, it'd be too late for anyone to find her.

Rylee scurried into the passenger seat and locked the doors. "Now would be a good time for you to bark," Rylee said, turning around and looking at Raisin. Of course, he wasn't barking, unlike the last five days where she'd done her best to keep him from barking at slamming doors and suitcases being lugged up and down stairs in the hotels.

The blue sports pickup maneuvered in front of her car. A colorful sticker, plastered on the back bumper, said: "Doug Mays for Cranberry Bay Mayor." A tall, broad-shouldered man stepped out of the truck. He wore jeans and heavy brown hiking boots and strode purposefully toward Rylee's car. Rain cascaded off his thick hooded black jacket. He tapped briefly on her window. "Everything okay?" he mouthed. "It's a nasty storm out here."

"I have a flat."

The man raised an eyebrow and shook his head.

He couldn't hear her. She'd have to take her chances and roll down the window. Thanking the age of her car, Rylee turned the old-fashioned window crank and yelled above the wind, "My left front tire is flat."

"I'll take a look. Do you have a spare?"

"In the trunk. I can help you ..." She knew how to change a tire. She didn't need this man to rescue her.

"I got it," the man hollered. "It's nasty out here. I'm already soaked. Stay there."

Rylee nodded. It was pouring rain, and she wasn't exactly dressed for changing a tire. Raisin paced on the backseat, and Rylee reached into his treat bag on the front seat. She held the small dog biscuit out to Raisin, and he gobbled it from her hand.

A sharp tap on the car window jerked Rylee's attention away from Raisin. The man's hood had fallen off, and his blond hair was wet. Rylee swallowed hard. Her eyes passed over his high forehead and the freckles that danced across his cheekbones. A flicker of recognition crossed his face at the same time as her heart fluttered. Bryan gazed back at her with all the kindness and compassion she once remembered.

Slowly, Rylee stepped out of the car as Raisin gave a sharp bark in the backseat. "It's okay, boy," Rylee said to

Raisin. She pressed her hands against the back of the car and leaned against it, trying to steady herself. The wet car soaked the back of her bare legs, but she barely felt it. Rain fell off her head and danced onto the gravel below her feet.

"Bryan," Rylee whispered. Her insides quivered from something that reached into her far deeper than the cold rain and wind. She didn't dare look at his hand to see the gold wedding band that claimed him as belonging to someone else. She tried to steady herself. She'd known it was a possibility to run into Bryan; Cranberry Bay wasn't that big. But nothing could have prepared her heart for the moment when it actually happened.

Bryan's eyes swept over her face, down her soaking wet cardigan, and to her red painted toenails peeking from the tips of her sandals. "Rylee?" A shadow flashed across his face. "I thought it was you … but I didn't …" Suddenly he cleared his throat. "Pop the trunk, and I'll get that spare on for you."

Rylee nodded and slipped into the driver's seat. She leaned down and lifted the trunk latch. Her hands shook as the old feelings for Bryan rushed through her.

Chapter Two

Bryan rolled under beside the car and positioned the spare tire in place. He lifted the tire onto the axle and gave it a hard twist, ensuring it was snug. A heavy lock of wet hair fell to his forehead, and he brushed it aside. Memories poured through his mind. Rylee sitting on the front porch swing, painting her toes red, and smiling at him. Rylee and her soft mouth that he couldn't stop kissing. Rylee, who had told him she loved him and promised to marry him, but left the next day, leaving his heart in pieces.

When the spare was firmly in place, Bryan rolled out from under the car. He walked to the driver's side.

Rylee rolled down the window, and he cleared his throat. "That should hold you until you get into Cranberry Bay. I'm sorry about your grandmother. Cranberry Bay will miss her."

"Thank you," Rylee said. "I always planned to return to see her. But I kept putting it off, things came up …" Rylee's voice softened to barely a whisper.

"Yes, well …" Bryan shifted and looked away from her and into the tall evergreens. Rain bounced off his shoulders and landed on the ground with soft splats. He wasn't sure if he was angry with himself for believing Rylee's words now or for the years he held on to the foolish belief that she'd come back to him and Cranberry Bay. He had tried everything he could to forget her, including marrying someone he didn't love. Nothing had worked.

"I imagine you won't find Cranberry Bay any different." Bryan repeatedly opened and closed his left hand. He quickly pocketed his hand and ran his finger over his empty ring finger. Nothing had changed in Cranberry Bay over the last ten years. Jobs were scarce and limited to clamming, forestry, and dairy farming. Summer tourists streamed past on the freeway, stopping only to grab an iced coffee or browse the antique shop before heading into the popular surrounding beach towns. Cranberry Bay was a stop for lunch on the way to somewhere else.

"I'm not planning to stay long. I'll clean out the house, sell it, and then I'm moving to San Diego," Rylee said firmly.

Bryan couldn't help but smile, faintly. Rylee was still the same, making plans for her life to run according to a set schedule. It'd been one of the things he loved about her. Every summer, she outlined a plan of hikes she wanted to take, crafts she wanted to make, and meals she wanted to cook. By the end of the summer, her plan was always complete. The only summer it hadn't been was the summer they fell in love. Instead of working through her plan, they'd spent long lazy days floating on the river and evenings exploring each other in the small river cottage. He often teased her about her summer plan, and she only smiled and said sometimes plans changed. He had loved nothing better than knowing he was a part of that plan-changing summer. If only it could have been forever.

"Thank you for fixing the tire." Rylee raised her eyes and met Bryan's. His heart pounded in his chest, the same way it always had when she looked at him, making him believe he had more to offer than he ever believed in himself. She'd always had that ability. A way to look at him or touch his arm and convince him he could do anything.

"Rylee ..." Bryan cleared his throat. There was so much he wanted to say to her. But a gust of wind blew into the trees above their head, and a large branch cracked. "Cranberry Bay is about ten-miles from here. Stay straight on the highway and I'll follow you into Cranberry Bay. The storm is pretty bad."

"Thank you," Rylee said and rolled up her window.

Slowly, she pulled out of the gravel and onto the highway.

Bryan strode to his truck and slipped inside. His pulse raced as a large tree branch dropped to the ground where Rylee's car had been parked. He put his truck in gear and pulled onto the highway. Mountain storms in the fall were not things to play with. His younger brother, Adam, worked as a forest ranger and had more than one harrowing story about a hiker who'd gotten trapped by falling trees.

Bryan flipped off the mystery audiobook he had been listening to and turned the station to rock. The heavy drumbeat filled his ears as he followed Rylee's car down the mountain highway. One of Rylee's taillights flickered and turned off. He made a mental note to fix that for her as soon as possible and hoped Sheriff Anderson was off-duty tonight. The sheriff looked for ways to make money and didn't think twice of ticketing cars for missing taillights. Bryan had gotten a few tickets himself, but he usually managed to finagle his way out of them by buying a couple rounds of microbrews at the pub.

Slowing to twenty-five, Bryan drove past the river marina in the gloom. A few fishing boats were tethered to the docks, and the pub lights glowed as the music of one of the popular beach bands poured through the open doors. They spent the off-season practicing new songs at the pub. Bryan sometimes grabbed his own guitar and joined in. He liked spending the long, dark, rainy evenings with many of the men whom he had known all his life.

Across from the marina, the city park overlooked the bay, and wooden benches dripped with rain. Heavy dark leaves covered the grass. In the fading light, the chipped paint on the buildings and the overgrown grass wasn't noticeable.

Bryan worked with a crew of high school kids to keep things tidy. The teens earned volunteer credits, and the city enjoyed a well-kept summer park. Once school started, he did the job with occasional help from a teen on a Saturday.

Ahead of him, Rylee made a left on Elm Street and her taillight faded out of sight. Bryan turned right, two streets away from Rylee's grandmother's house, and continued past the town's two-story, brick elementary school and the gymnasium in the playground that his Dad had helped build years ago. The PTA never had funding to replace the old set with a new one, and a couple of the swings were missing. Half a block past the playground, Bryan turned left onto an asphalt-paved driveway. He slowly pulled up behind the Jeep Grand Cherokee belonging to his older brother, Sawyer, and the four-door black Honda CRV belonging to his younger brother, Adam. The garage door stood open, and his Mom's small, silver Toyota was nestled inside beside a shelving unit filled with plastic bins of Christmas decorations.

The home was like the other two-story Craftsman homes on the street. When he was eleven, Dad hired a couple guys to build a dormer on the back. Dad joked about never being able to get the loan paid off before he retired, but six months after the dormer was finished, Dad suddenly passed away of a heart attack. His generous life-insurance policy not only paid off the dormer but also the rest of the mortgage, giving Rebecca Shuster and her two boys and her twins a place to call home, worry-free.

Bryan kicked aside large piles of leaves as he headed up the walkway. The gingham living room curtains stood open, and golden lamplight blazed into the dark and rainy night. A steady trail of water drained off the roof into a large puddle. He made a mental note to stop by and check the gutter tomorrow. A large pine tree hung over the house and dropped needles onto the roof. The needles easily clogged the gutters and caused damage to the cedar siding if left unchecked.

A glowing carved pumpkin sat on the front porch step, and Bryan smiled. Yesterday, when he stopped by to see about a leaky toilet in the downstairs bathroom, the pumpkin hadn't been carved. Tonight, candlelight shone from a stenciled nose, mouth, and pair of lopsided eyes. A plastic carving tool lay across the front porch by the pumpkin. Bryan leaned down and picked up the knife.

He opened the front door, and the smell of pot roast wafted through the room, which was painted bright yellow. A fire crackled in the fireplace, and Adam leaned against the stone mantel.

"We were ready to eat without you." Adam's dark, thick heavy hair lay across his forehead in a mass of curls. He wore dark jeans and a flannel shirt, unbuttoned three buttons so his white undershirt poked through. He'd kicked off his usual heavy boots, and his large feet in black-and-gray flannel socks shifted on the hardwood floor.

"Sorry I'm late." Bryan said. "It was a long trip back from Portland."

Sawyer uncrossed his legs and stood up from a plush, leather reclining chair. He drained the last of his beer and nodded to Brian. "There are more drinks in the fridge."

"Thanks," Bryan said. "I think I'll go see if Mom needs any help." Sawyer had never been a big drinker, but ever since his beloved wife had died of cancer, he had a habit of making sure there was enough alcohol flowing to keep the pain away.

It didn't surprise Bryan to find both his brothers lounging in the living room while Mom cooked dinner. After Dad died, each brother played a different part in the family. He helped Mom in the house. Sawyer contributed money when Mom needed a little extra, and Adam helped by driving Mom the hour-and-a-half over the mountains to Portland for appointments and shopping trips to purchase bulk household items. It was unspoken between the three of them that they would take care of Mom.

Bryan kicked off his mud-splattered shoes and left them lying at the front door with Adam's work boots. A small pair of pink tennis shoes lay, upside down, on top of Sawyer's dress shoes. He smiled at his niece Lauren's haphazard way of making sure her Dad didn't forget to take her home, too. Not that Sawyer had any thought of leaving his daughter behind. He loved her fiercely and would do anything for his little girl.

Bryan's socked feet padded against the hardwood floor as he passed the wall in the hallway filled with family photos. Bryan's left shoulder brushed against a small gold frame and tilted the picture. In the picture, he and his twin sister, Lisa, stood by a green canoe that was alongside a river. Lisa was the only one of the Shuster siblings who had left Cranberry Bay. She had married a fisherman from Seattle and took a job working as a public relations director at a children's hospital. A few years into the marriage, Frank died at sea during a fishing trip to Alaska, leaving Lisa to raise their daughter, Maddie. She often declined invitations to come home at the holidays, saying she was needed too much by the families at the hospital. Bryan understood Lisa's commitment to her work, but he missed his twin and niece and wished they lived closer.

Bryan averted his eyes from the last picture on the wall. A framed photo of Dad and his sister and brothers gathered in a large circle around a canoe. Bryan stood a small distance away from all of them with a scowl on his face. The camping trip had been only one more time he didn't please Dad.

Bryan headed into the kitchen where Mom chopped plump tomatoes at a wooden cutting board beside the sink. Lauren perched on a stool and dropped pieces of lettuce into salad bowls. She wore jeans and a blue sweatshirt with Eagles stenciled across the front. Clasped in a high ponytail, her curly blonde hair swung with every move.

"Let me do that, Mom." Bryan stepped up behind her and took the knife out of her hands. "We'll finish up, right Lauren?"

Lauren hopped down from the stool. She pushed her bangs out of her eyes, but they flopped back down in the same place again. "Grandma let me carve the pumpkin today."

"I know." Bryan held up the plastic knife. "You left the knife on the porch."

"Sorry!" Lauren jumped over and yanked the utensil from Bryan's hand. She twirled across the kitchen, opened the pantry door, and dropped it into the trash can.

Rebecca grabbed a red-and-blue hot pad, and, opening the oven, pulled out the steaming pot roast. She carried it to the counter and set it on a hot plate. "I think we're all set." Rebecca wiped her hands on an orange-and-black ruffled apron. She nodded toward the dining room table, set with the family's blue-and-white dinnerware set.

"Smells great." Sawyer strolled into the kitchen and ruffled his daughter's hair. "Time to put the ice in the glasses," he instructed her.

Obediently, Lauren opened the lower freezer drawer and pulled out the bin of ice. She grabbed a set of plastic tongs and headed into the dining room.

Sawyer dropped his empty bottle of beer into the recycling bin by the backdoor and looked into the dark backyard. "How's business, Bryan?" Sawyer whirled around, and his brown eyes met Bryan's. "Sold any houses yet?"

"I'm working on it." Bryan fisted his hands. Eight years ago, Sawyer had gotten a lucky break when he was hired to be the developer of a premier community at the beach. The houses sold quickly, but instead of continuing to buy property, Sawyer bought ten acres on the outskirts of town and built his own home. During the housing crash, Sawyer had money in the bank and nothing in land. While developers around him fell, Sawyer slowly bought up property at rock bottom prices. Now, he owned what seemed like half the county and had accounts large enough to buy another country estate, something he never stopped reminding Bryan, who hadn't been as lucky as his older brother in business.

Rebecca reached behind her and untied her apron. "Jack mentioned he's handling Ellen Harper's estate for her granddaughter, Rylee. I suspect they will need a real estate agent for the sale."

She smiled at Bryan. Jack Perkins had been a longtime family friend. A widow for the last five years, he and Rebecca spent more and more time together. Both of them waved off all discussion of romance.

"Rylee Harper." Sawyer leaned against the counter. He crossed his arms over his chest and studied Bryan. "Kinda remember you wanted to marry her ..."

"Yes." Bryan grabbed a plate, loaded it with roast beef, and carried it to the table. "Childhood fantasy." He pulled out a chair and sat down beside Adam, hoping Sawyer would let the conversation drop.

"She might have made the best decision to leave Cranberry Bay." Sawyer moved a heavy oak chair, straightening the paisley cushion. He sat down opposite him. "The School Board is talking about closing the elementary school and sending the kids to the coast elementary, twenty miles away."

"Closing the elementary school?" Bryan dropped his fork to the plate with a thud. How could they close the elementary school and tear it down? The school hosted annual carnival fund-raisers, children's art workshops, and community education classes on everything from cooking to hiking to dog training. If the school was closed and torn down, everything would stop. There was nowhere else in the town big enough to hold the community events.

"Shh ..." Sawyer raised his finger to his lips as Lauren danced into the dining room. She balanced her plate in one hand and a glass of milk in the other.

"Probably won't happen right away," Sawyer said, eying Lauren as she sank into a chair on the other side of him. "But people are concerned. Families are dwindling, and the school has lost a lot of funding without the tax base here. The district thinks it'd be better to combine some schools."

Bryan picked up his napkin and set it in his lap. "I might have a solution for Cranberry Bay." He took a bite of his salad as his brothers turned to him. Bryan smiled, enjoying the moment of attention from his family. Most of the time, it was his brothers who held the center stage, not him.

"And ..." Adam asked, scooping a heaping spoonful of mashed potatoes onto his plate.

"I met with a seller in Portland today. He's selling a couple of riverboats. A casino and a hotel. I'd like to buy them and begin to bring tourism back to Cranberry Bay. If we could build up our travel and tourism revenue, we'd be able to offer jobs and be eligible for some of the state tax money that the beach towns enjoy. We could be much more than a stop-through on the way to somewhere else, if we had something for people to do and a reason to stay for a night or two."

"That's a fabulous idea." Ellen leaned over and set a steaming bowl of vegetables on the table. She took her seat at the head of the table and briefly smiled at each of the brothers and Lauren.

"Have you talked to the bank about securing a loan?" Adam asked. "I've heard it's still hard to get financing for commercial real estate."

"The lending restrictions are still tight." Bryan ran his fingers over the etched glass filled with water. He didn't tell his brothers that his own lack of a steady job history, combined with not owning his own home hadn't won him any points at the bank. A few years ago, during his divorce, he'd given everything to Amy, knowing the reason for their marriage failing was his inability to let go of Rylee Harper. Amy had immediately sold the house and moved to Portland, where he heard she'd remarried and had two children.

"I'm hoping to gather some funding from people who might be interested in sponsoring the project."

Sawyer lowered his fork and studied Bryan. "Funding isn't going to be easy to find in Cranberry Bay. Most people can barely keep the lights on."

Bryan fisted his left hand at his side. Sawyer's words traveled to his gut and stuck there, like something he'd eaten that hadn't agreed with him. "You got any other options?"

"It sounds like a worthwhile proposition, and one I might be interested in funding. But..."

"But ..." Bryan gazed at Sawyer, feeling as if he'd been hurled back to their years of childhood board-game nights where Sawyer always won. Game shark, the family called him. Everything was a game to Sawyer, and nine times out of ten, he won.

"But you know how I like a game ..."

Bryan's stomach clenched. He knew all too well about Sawyer's bets. He'd watched him over the years offer bets to people and laugh about them when they lost. But he was running out of options and time quickly. "What is your game this time?"

"I'll give you the full funding for the riverboats, but ..." Sawyer paused and eyed him, obviously relishing in the power he held over his younger brother, "you have to convince Rylee Harper to move to Cranberry Bay. She can sell her grandmother's home or not. But she has to decide she loves Cranberry Bay so much that she'll live here full time. If you can convince Rylee to move to Cranberry Bay, then I will know you can convince anyone to move here."

"And, how do you propose I do that?" Bryan asked, pressure building in his stomach at the thought of Rylee

Harper living in Cranberry Bay for good. She'd never agree to it, and if she did, how would he handle seeing her everyday around town? He had barely been able to contain his emotions at seeing her on the dark and wet highway. The town was too small for them not to bump into each other on a regular basis.

Sawyer leaned back in his chair. "That is up to you to figure out."

Bryan licked his lips. His mouth tasted dry. "You know Rylee and I are never going to be together. That's over." The words felt like lies on his tongue, and he forced them out. He and Rylee were over. She'd made that clear the morning he found her note telling him she'd returned to Las Vegas. He'd tried to contact her a couple times, but each time, her phone went only to voice mail. As the weeks turned into months, his hope of her returning dwindled, and, finally, he'd done the only thing he knew how to do to get over her; He married someone else. The marriage had lasted only eighteen months, and he had never forgotten Rylee Harper.

Sawyer bit into a small tomato. He shrugged. "I don't really care what you and Rylee Harper do or don't do."

"Then why are you setting up this bet about her?"

"Because ..." Sawyer placed his hands on the table and leaned forward, "I'd offer you the money, but I know you'll never take it without a challenge. You like the challenge, and Rylee Harper is the best challenge I see right now. She is the perfect candidate for convincing that Cranberry Bay has something to offer."

Bryan forked a piece of meat. His head pounded. He'd never win the bet. Rylee had no intention of staying in Cranberry Bay. She made that clear today. She had no more desire to stay in Cranberry Bay today than she did ten years ago when she left and broke his heart. But he also needed money. He needed a way to save Cranberry Bay and prove to the town and himself he could be what his Dad had claimed he couldn't be—a success. The bank wouldn't give him the loan, and time was ticking. If he didn't do something, the town that he'd grown up in, the people he cared about, and the place he loved would become nonexistent. He could not allow that to happen.

Lauren leaned over to him. "Are they closing my school? Please don't let them close it."

Bryan gazed into his niece's pleading eyes. She'd already lost so much when her Mom died of cancer; he couldn't allow her to lose her elementary school too. Not when he could do something to save the town.

Bryan jerked his head back up and stared at Sawyer. "Game on." He would find a way to convince Rylee Harper to stay without allowing his heart to be shattered.

To read more of *Sweetheart Cottage*, please go to your favorite bookstore.

www.ingramcontent.com/pod-product-compliance
Lightning Source LLC
Chambersburg PA
CBHW060226180626
46813CB00007B/2977